AFFAIR WITH A
LOG CABIN

DIVEN

By
LARREN WOOD

Library of Congress
Catalog Card Number: 94-61686
ISBN # 09636546-2-4

Printed in U.S.A.

FOREWORD

I have the somewhat dubious distinction of sharing three different log cabins with three different husbands. While I may quip that my devotion to log cabins outlives my devotion to any husband, herein lies the story of my devotion to them all.

I refer to my husbands with pseudonyms. I do it only to protect their privacy. They are fine, honorable men who I feel fortunate to have shared my life with. While two of my marriages ended in divorce, my feelings of respect and admiration for the men will endure throughout my lifetime.

The storyteller in me tends to exaggeration and embellishment for the sake of entertainment. It shall remain the reader's responsibility to distinguish between entertainment and reality. For the benefit of anyone who entertains the idea of building their own log home, I did not embellish the "chicken wire & fiberglass insulation" process. It was entirely as distasteful as I made it out to be. Modern builder's methods and materials are much improved today.

A cynic once said a first marriage is for love, a second for practicality and a third for companionship. Having the basis for comparison has not provided me any newfound insights on the subject. I shared my youth and my babies with "Ace". Together we fulfilled a dream of building our own log home. The "engineer" introduced me to northern Minnesota, my resorting lifestyle and his German heritage. We experienced a variety of cultures and travel from Mexico to Canada. The "professor" shares my middle age, my grandchildren and my dreams for the future. He tolerates my persnickety ways, my writing and my resorting. He encourages me to fly as far and as high as I am able. I know he will catch me if I fall.

"Affair With a Log Cabin" is a story of a transplanted Southern girl at heart. It is a story of a devotion to a way of life, a heritage and the log cabins that symbolize that heritage. It is a story of struggle, of winning and losing and of keeping a sense of humor through it all.

When I was thirty, I expected to gain wisdom and a profound philosophy regarding life's perils and pitfalls by the time I was forty. When I was forty, I was too deeply embroiled in life's perils and pitfalls to contemplate wisdom and philosophy. Wisdom was postponed until I was fifty. When I was fifty, notions of philosophy were long since forgotten. Instead of wisdom, I collect sunsets and pick more daisies. Perhaps, therein lies wisdom after all.

DEDICATION

Dedicated to "Ace" and our daughters,

Desmon Johnson
and
Diane Bucci

With many fond memories of a log cabin
at the top of "Spindly Pines Drive".

AFFAIR WITH A LOG CABIN

Part I

Chapter 1

SOUTHERN ROOTS

Growing up on an Oklahoma farm during the 50's was about as exciting as watching paint dry. Being a girl with a yen for a more romantic existence, I began to plot my escape from the farm early on. The summer of my twelfth birthday marked the beginning of my romantic era. The era never ended.

There were four of us and usually five. Besides me, there was my brother who arrived when I was three years old, my parents and usually my mother's daddy. We lived modestly as small crop farmers did. We were happy and healthy and didn't ask much more.

My earliest memories are of listening to Ma Perkins, Stella Dallas, Just Plain Bill and the continuing saga of Pepper Young's family on the radio. That was before modern psychology determined that listening to soap operas was bad for three-year olds. Of course they weren't called soap operas back then. They were daytime serial dramas. I listened with the same rapt attention as my mother. Apparently it did me no great harm. My only recall of the subject matter is the announcer admonishing us to tune in tomorrow. We always did.

Mother's philosophy regarding child-rearing included a proverb to fit any and all occasions. Many of her sayings sounded downright biblical. She delivered them with such an air of authority that we never questioned her source. Whatever their origin, they made a lasting impression and served me well throughout my life.

The proverb Mother lived by was, "The Lord helps those who help themselves." My daddy was of Scotch/Irish descent and not always in total agreement with my mother. His motto was, "Never do today what you can put off until tomorrow." He said she would have worked us all to death if we'd have just let her. He wasn't about to let her.

My favorite of Mother's quotes was usually directed at my persnickety nature.

"Now, Larren, you will catch more
flies with honey than vinegar."

A close second was along the same line of reasoning.

"Now, Larren, don't cut off your nose
to spite your face."

I firmly believe the, "Now, Larren", preface bought her the time she needed to select the most fitting proverb to suit the occasion. If I heard them once, I heard them a thousand times. They became the code I lived by for years to come.

I subscribed to a few of her others.

"Pretty is as pretty does."

"Youth is beauty."

"Be sure to put on clean underwear in case you are in an accident."

After many years of accident-free living, I challenged her research and discarded that one.

"If you eat too much salt, it will dry up your blood."

"If you cross your eyes, they will stick that way."

"If you stand on your head, your liver will turn over."

My mother was obviously ahead of her time when it came to body parts.

"Look before you leap."

I never did learn when to apply that one. I always leaped before I remembered it.

Mother's proverbs shaped my brother and me into God-fearing, law abiding citizens. We never knew which of her proverbs came from the Bible, which were the State's laws and which were original. It didn't seem prudent to question. She delivered each and every one of them with the fire and brimstone of a Southern Baptist preacher converting sinners to saints.

"Do unto others as you would have them do unto you".

"You reap what you sow."

"The chickens will always come home to roost."

"When you misbehave, I don't have to punish you. The LORD will punish you!"

Just try to get away from that one. Every time I skinned a knee or took a tumble, I figured it was the Lord evening the score with me for tormenting my baby brother.

If her proverbs didn't get you, her homemade lye soap surely would. My mother was a fanatic when it came to scrubbing. It's a wonder we survived her Saturday morning, going-to-town baths and shampoos. I can tell you they were quite a production. Mother started the preparations the day before. She polished our shoes, starched and ironed our clothes and rolled

10

my hair up in rag strings which I slept in. The resulting curls were a mix of friz and string. Friday nights I slept fitfully, tossing and turning on the hard knots of the rag curls. After the lye soap shampoo, sleeping on the rag knots and the string/friz comb-out, my head was sore until the next Friday when we did it all over again.

Looking back, I suppose we were poor. I wasn't aware of it at the time. Mother always said we were middle class. I had as much as any of my friends and a lot more than some. I knew there were people who were worse off than we were. I never wondered about those who might have been better. We had plenty to eat and wear. Mother sometimes sewed my dresses from printed flour sacks, two sacks to a dress. I was allowed to select the flour sacks off the grocery shelf. After we bought one especially pretty sack, I kept an eye on the flour shelf for weeks - looking for a matching sack. The sack had a white background sprigged with little, brown deer wearing pink bows around their necks. The subsequent sacks had deer with yellow bows tied around their necks. Mother said it wouldn't look right to mix and match.

When I was twelve, my world included a menagerie of farm animals and haylofts which the town kids envied. I felt deprived of their many social activities. To my way of thinking, I was missing out on life's finer things. I would be forever branded a "farm kid" in the social register. I wasn't sure what the social register was, but whoever was in charge of it most certainly lived in town. I thought it was probably connected to the

McIntosh County Democrat society column which I scrutinized each Thursday in pursuit of a more meaningful life. I read of bridge parties and country club affairs. I figured out who was the "Who's Who" in our small town society.

As the dog days of my twelfth summer dragged on, I fantasized a romantic future in a distant Southern city. When the August days grew hotter and hotter, my fantasy world became increasingly grandiose. In my mind I was cool and shaded by magnificent live oak trees adorned with delicate Spanish moss. In reality it was cotton picking time. How I hated picking cotton! I would do anything to get out of picking cotton. I dawdled between the cotton rows, daydreaming and lagging behind the other pickers. At weighing time my picking sack was never more than half full. By the end of picking season I had created a romantic Southern past for myself as well. I hounded older and wiser relatives for forgotten details of my Harding family history. In my imagination I embellished the facts. For each long, hot summer after that, my Southern heritage continued to grow.

The year I turned fourteen (after three showings of "Gone With the Wind" at the Gentry Theater) I narrowed the cast of characters to the paternal side of my family. My daddy was the youngest of twelve children and sprang from Southern roots. While both my grandparents were well into their 70's when I was born, my grandmother lived another twenty years to provide details of my Virginia ancestors.

Rachel Isetta (Cox) Harding was a feisty Southern Belle, even during her 90's. She was the only "lady" I knew with pierced ears. In my adolescent wisdom I regarded pierced ears as a sign of questionable morals, flaunted by women of the streets. I have yet to trace the foundation for that premise, but it served me well for at least ten years. Since my Grandmother Rachel was most certainly a lady, I surmised that the cultural differences between Oklahoma and Virginia explained the gold studs adorning her earlobes. Her fine, white hair was secured in a twist with tortoise shell combs. Her dresses were long-sleeved, mid-calf, modest frocks. They all appeared to be cut from the same pattern in a variety of fabrics. I rarely saw her dress when it wasn't protected by an apron. I never saw her legs when they weren't protected by long, brown cotton stockings. Of course my grandmother didn't have "legs". She had "limbs". Sensible, black laced shoes completed her attire. Whenever she left her house, she wore a hat and carried gloves. She was most certainly a lady.

My grandfather, Embrer Richard Harding, was as fine a Southern gentleman as you'd ever hope to meet. It was his family heritage that I proudly embellished. He was the family patriarch, even after his sight failed him. He was the only blind man I knew. He spent his days sitting in a bedroom by a flower garden. Strings tied along the trees guided his daily walks. His soft, Southern drawl was a delight to hear. The melody was more suited to a Virginia plantation than an Oklahoma farm. When we went to visit, my daddy always took him a bottle of "sippin' whiskey" for medicinal purposes - despite the State's prohibition laws and Mother's proverbs.

I was one of the last grandchildren he was able to see. When my baby brother was born, Mother put him in our grandad's arms. Grandad saw him with his fingers. He slowly felt my baby brother's chubby arms and legs, chuckled happily and gave my mother his patriarchal approval.

The earliest story I remember hearing from Grandmother Rachel related the birth of my daddy when she was forty-seven years old. When her waistline began to expand, she feared she had a tumor. When the tumor started kicking, she collapsed at the foot of the family staircase. She laughed awhile and cried awhile, laughed some more and cried some more. She couldn't decide which was the least desirable - a potentially fatal tumor or a twelfth child. That story led to stories of eleven other babies. During some of the births her only assistance was a Negro woman, a freed slave who had chosen to stay on in the only home she knew. Sometimes my grandmother would not see another white woman for months at a time. Her companion, nurse and friend was called "Mammy" by her children. While the word "plantation" was never used, I heard stories of Virginia ancestors who were tobacco farmers and slave owners. I longed for hoop skirts, plantation balls and the Antebellum South of Scarlett O'Hara. I grieved that history had misplaced me so far from my roots.

The summer I turned fifteen, my thoughts were more often on boys than my Southern heritage. I continued to focus on hoop skirts and crinolines since that was the current style. At times I grappled with six or seven petticoats a wearing. The heat and humidity wilted the stiffest of petticoat parchment. Not to be outdone by circumstance, my outermost petticoat was fitted with a metal hoop at the hem. The underlying layers of net supported an illusion of pure fluff. I remember sitting in a stifling, August classroom - comparing myself to that frothy layer of petticoats concealing the rigid hoop. I wondered how many acquaintances perceived past the fluff of my illusion. My yards of petticoats and skirts were mid-calf, waistlines were wasplike and necklines scooped to reveal the beginning of cleavage. It was as close as I ever came to being a Southern Belle.

While my paternal family roots spoke of gentility, my mother's daddy was my most beloved companion. As far back as I could remember, he had lived in our house. At least he lived with us after his many short-lived marriages. He was the only person I knew who had been married five times and lived most of his life single. His marriages usually had a basis in practicality rather than romance. The love of his life (Rema, my mother's mother) died at an early age. Alone, he took care of the two little girls she left him.

Instead of the frilly dresses commonly worn by little girls in those days, he dressed my mother and her sister in matching, brown coveralls. Instead of the rag string curls I suffered, he bobbed their hair short. He washed their clothes by hand in a black, iron kettle. Scrubbing the clothes, the house and everything in it was a job he took most seriously. I knew full well where Mother came by her love for lye soap!

On several occasions the three of them traveled across the country in a Model-T Ford. My mother told stories of train rides to North Carolina and the beauty of the Blue Ridge and Great Smoky Mountains. Her entire childhood sounded like a gypsy camp. I thought she must have had the most exciting life and envied her many adventures.

From time to time, Grandad married to provide a step-mother for his daughters. His marriages never lasted and I never knew his wives. When he married for the last time during my high school years, I finally took note of his romantic side.

My grandad, Ervin Sardis Messer, came from the Blue Ridge Mountains of North Carolina. He was small in stature among brothers who towered over him. I never knew his family. It was only through his eyes that I saw the hill country people who were my ancestors. Judging from his demeanor and style, the term "hillbilly" was as good a description as any.

True to his heritage, Grandad always had to have a good coon dog. Apparently his judgement regarding what entailed a good coon dog was a bit flawed. Daddy was forever complaining about Grandad's current coon dog. They always seemed to be in some sort of trouble. Either they chased the chickens or sucked eggs or were just plain sorry. They were all named "Pup". I recall at least a dozen "Pups". Some were blue tick hounds and some were red-speckled bird dogs. According to Grandad, each and every one of them was a good coon dog. On one of Grandad's coon hunts he got a little over anxious and stuck his hand in a hollow tree where a full-grown raccoon was holed up. The coon chewed him up pretty good. It was one of the few times in his life that Grandad went to a doctor. The bandage hampered his coon hunting for awhile. Grandad never weighed more than 130 pounds dripping wet. His face was always tanned from working in the sun, except for the top of his head which was white under his cap. It was bald and covered by hair which he grew long on the sides to lap over the top. He wore blue denim work clothes and a feedstore cap cocked at an angle just framing the clearest blue eyes I have ever seen.

Much to Mother's consternation, Grandad refused to wear his dentures except when he ate. According to him, why else would he need to? The ill-fitting dentures were wrapped in a handkerchief and stuffed in his shirt pocket. He dipped snuff from a small, silver can with the blade of his pocketknife. The snuff mixed with saliva and settled in brown creases at the corners of his mouth. I avoided his dreaded spitcan lest I spill the contents. When he died in his nineties, the most precious remembrance I kept was his shiny, silver snuff can.

Mother always seemed to be setting Grandad up in housekeeping. About the time she got him all settled

17

in, wanderlust would overtake him. He would pack his tartan-plaid, cardboard suitcase and head for North Carolina to visit relatives and a previous wife. The cardboard suitcase held many treasures including a pair of gray, felt spats. I never saw him wear the spats except in pictures taken fifty years earlier. They looked most sporting above his brown and white saddle shoes. He was quite dapper in the days before my grandmother died. I wondered if the spats reminded him of her. He lost the suitcase and the spats on one of his trips. I felt I had lost an important piece of my heritage.

While my Harding relatives spoke of a gracious Southern lifestyle, the Messer side of the family was more colorful. They grew tobacco as well, but not in plantation style. My Great-Grandmother Messer grew tobacco in her garden patch. She cured the leaves into little twists which she chewed herself. Great Great-Grandmother Sleuder smoked a corncob pipe. This was hardy stock I sprang from! I swapped gentility for hillbilly yearnings. I dreamed of log cabins, moonshine whiskey and good coon dogs. Either way, I was Southern bred and proud of it. The strains of "Dixie" hummed in my mind.

Grandad Messer's conversation was peppered with hillbilly expressions and colloquial mispronunciation. Somehow I always knew it was his personal vocabulary and not to be imitated. His favorite verb was "hain't" as in "I hain't got no more snuff." Like my mother, he quoted proverbs to live by. Perhaps he was the source of her profound wisdom. His advice I recall most often is, "Thar's more'n one way to skin a cat, Sis." And indeed, there always was.

Often the "cat I had to skin" took the form of a Saturday night date. During the fifties, a girl caught sitting home on a Saturday night might as well give up any dreams she might have had for a future. It was a fate worse than death itself. If the girl was past the age of sixteen, she was well on her way to ending up an old maid.

Where dating was concerned, the farm boys were at a decided disadvantage - since the number of farm boys with a car was virtually nil. The family transportation which they were able to borrow usually smelled like a hog truck (which it usually was). Sitting through a drive-in movie on a hot, summer night in a hog truck did not usually lead to a second date. Therefore, all eyes were directed to the town boys. The spirit of competition was keen amongst us. My biggest coup was during my junior year of high school. I landed a football player with his own red, Chevy convertible. His parents belonged to the Muskogee Country Club. No matter what successes I was to achieve during my lifetime, they could only be considered minor in comparison.

Like the rest of my generation, I had one foot in the past and the other foot not quite sure where to set itself. We were before Woodstock and Vietnam - not exactly flower children, but a bit to the left of tradition.

James Dean was our idol in "Rebel Without a Cause". Elvis Presley was our hero. We weren't as much concerned with world issues as we were in acquiring a husband. We schemed, primped, flirted and connived to that end. We knew the way to a man's heart was through his stomach and that good Southern cooking was the key to success in life. We learned to bake biscuits, make cream gravy, chicken-fry steak and cultivate a speaking style that dripped honey. All we ever needed to know we learned in our mother's kitchen.

Just to keep the record straight regarding my Southern culture, it should be noted that feminine charm was never a substitute for brains. It's just that we learned early on when to flaunt what.

Chapter 2

MARRIAGE AND LOVE AFFAIRS

It didn't take long to find the husband of my dreams, the man I will call "Ace". I married my college sweetheart just after my nineteenth birthday. Actually, he was Ace the III. His grandfather was Ace, Sr. and his father was Ace, Jr. His grandfather hailed from Valdosta, Georgia and spoke with the same quiet grace that mine did. He was primarily concerned that I was not a distant relative of Warren G. Harding. The late president's politics had not agreed with his.

Ace III was a star athlete on both the college basketball and baseball teams. He was no dumb jock and majored in mathematics. He planned to become a high school math teacher and coach state champion athletic teams. He played sports while I played house.

By the time Ace graduated from college, we were the proud parents of a beautiful baby girl. I named her Desmon after the heroine in a love story set in the South. Two years later we had Diane, named after my most beautiful sorority sister.

I was knee deep in Southern cooking along with baby diapers. I can tell you it wasn't always what it was cracked up to be. I was creating a few proverbs of my own. Most are unprintable.

After teaching for three years, Ace received a grant for his master's degree at the University of Arkansas in Fayetteville. We packed up our little family and moved to the hill country of the Ozarks. Chicken farms and apple orchards dotted the rolling hillsides. The autumn landscape was breathtaking. Quaint log cabins set among the Oak and Shortleaf Pine stole my heart.

At year's end we returned to Oklahoma and built our first home - a three-bedroom brick bungalow - not quite as picturesque as a mountain log cabin or as grand as Scarlett O'Hara's Tara. I should emphasize that we contracted for the building of the house. While Ace excelled in many areas, building was not one of them. His total woodworking experience was refinishing an antique rolltop desk. (This should be noted as a preface to the following chapters.)

As they say, you can't keep a good man down. After another year of teaching, Ace was looking for higher mountains to climb. We were off to the New Jersey shore for a position at Bell Laboratories. Life in New Jersey was an education for us all. We learned to omit "you all" from our vocabulary. It was a painful process. I should hasten to add that Okies do not use the term, "You all come back now", if only one person is involved. There has to be two people to include the "all". Yankees never seem to understand that. We also use two distinct words, "you all" instead of "y'all". This is one of the finer points that distinguishes an Okie from a Georgian.

I found a lot to love on the East Coast - horse farms set in rolling hills, rugged seashore and log cabins that had stood since the Revolutionary War. The weathered logs bleached gray, dovetailed in square corners and chinked with mud were the most beautiful pieces of art I had ever encountered. Perhaps it was their solid authenticity I loved more than their design. Homesickness overwhelmed me at times. While I had yet to live in a log cabin, these two-hundred year old houses felt like my home.

Our first Christmas in New Jersey was one of my most memorable. Holidays had always been a time for family and friends. I was feeling misplaced as I went through the motions of festive preparation. On Christmas Eve, I looked out the window of our garden apartment to see the mailman toting a large bundle up our walk. Behind him trailed at least half a dozen dogs, all sniffing and yapping at the bulky parcel. The tired Yankee postman failed to see the humor in the situation. He grumbled as I accepted the package from my parents. Gifts from them were already under our Christmas tree. I couldn't imagine what the fragrant box held inside. The contents were beyond my wildest dreams! Lovingly wrapped in the McIntosh County Democrat society column was a homegrown, home-cured ham all the way from Oklahoma. It was the best present I ever received.

The East Coast held a variety of new experiences for our family. It was, however, just a nice place to visit. We didn't want to live there forever. By the end of our second year, Ace's opportunity to advance the corporate ladder took us to Denver, Colorado. The move to Denver was the beginning of many changes. The mountain ethnic sneaked into our home a bit at a time. The first outward sign was in our footwear. We made a major financial investment in four pairs of lugsoled hiking boots that weighed ten pounds apiece. Lined up at the door, they closely resembled an item of furniture.

The daughters began to take on different personalities than we had known. The eldest became the "actress", the youngest was the "athlete". The actress began to climb the social ladder. The athlete ran track and played volleyball. The parents cast an eye toward the mountains to the west. Week-ends were spent scrutinizing realtor's ads and looking at mountain property. Our Chevy Vega station wagon was pushed to the limit if we went farther than the foothills.

Once started there was no turning back. We were into proverbs in a big way.

"Go west, young man, go west."

"Climb every mountain."

They became our anthem as we pushed farther and farther toward the Rockies. It was fortunate that realtors often provided the transportation, since the Vega always balked at the 6,000 foot mark. It would climb slower and slower until it finally heaved a sigh and said, "No more." Then we would put the lugsoles to the Rockies and hike on to whatever piece of mountain we were off to see. Needless to say, we had to be tenacious to continue our pursuit of the mountain life.

A major addition to our household was a true mountain dog, a St. Bernard named Aspen. Any family contemplating living above 6,000 feet should certainly have a St. Bernard in case they are ever caught in an avalanche. Our daughters realized this early on and set their hearts on a St. Bernard puppy. We never made it past a pet store window without oohing and ahhing over the pudgy, loveable balls of fur. Since the price tags on the balls of fur were in the $300-$400 range, Ace and I postponed the purchase. We were truly blessed when we were given a four-year old St. Bernard with a past. This was not the blessing the daughters had hoped for. The fully-grown Aspen resembled a small horse. Ace tried to pass her off as a six-month old puppy, explaining that St. Bernard puppies grow at a remarkable rate.

There was some doubt as to the details of Aspen's past, however it left scars. The outward sign of the scars was an intense fear of loud noises. Whenever thunder began to rumble from the mountains to the west, Aspen would quake with fright and make a mad dash for her hiding place under a bed. If she happened to be outside the house at the first sound of thunder, any and all doors were of little deterrence in her flight for safety.

While the generous person who gave us Aspen said that obedience training was also a part of her past, the only outward sign of that was her ability to shake hands. It was the only thing she ever learned. Since the only thing we required of Aspen was that she be around in case of an avalanche, her training was sufficient. The biggest problem with Aspen was that she filled up the Vega wagon all by herself. She jumped in the car the minute the door was opened, leaving no room for a driver or other passengers. Still, you knew she'd be right there at the first sign of an avalanche if she just had a bed to hide under.

I should emphasize that our weekly excursions with real estate agents were spent looking at bare mountain property - bare except for trees, that is. We had determined early on that the only way our budget could be stretched to include a mountain home was if we built it ourselves. Considering our past experience with building contractors and Ace's on the job training with the roll-top desk, we felt qualified to take on such a project. Let me tell you, that roll-top desk was no small undertaking. Our entire household was in a state of upheaval for months during the refurbishing of the roll-top alone. It most certainly qualified one to build a house.

Our pursuit of real estate spanned several seasons. The deep, winter snow hampered many a planned excursion. When we finally found a plot of land we could afford to buy, it was covered with five feet of the white stuff. It was also located at an altitude over 8,000 feet. Needless to say, the Vega had never been near it. Our land was beautiful with its stands of pine and aspen rising above the pristine whiteness of the snow. It included five acres of land which backed up to an abandoned roadbed, making a perfect sledding hill. We cut a Christmas tree from our new property and felt like the Walton family dragging it the two miles down the hill to the waiting Vega. With the St. Bernard, the tree on the top and the four of us, the Vega was pushed to the limit going downhill. We coasted into Denver.

Christmas was beautiful that year. We were knee deep in house plans by then. We planned to break ground with the spring thaw. Our stacks of house designs were not what you'd call "architect's originals". The least painful way to go was with what we called a "kit house". These were standard plans offered by several builders, with the wood cut at the factory, joists assembled and trucked to the lot where it was to be erected. Our mountain had several of the kit houses in various stages of owner construction. Many of them were still at the stage where they had been unloaded on the lots in earlier years, never to be assembled. The owners had either run out of money or energy and abandoned their dream early on. The piles of kit houses served as homes for various four-legged mountain creatures. We vowed that our home would never be among them.

Winter dragged on. Each week-end we loaded up the kids, dog and sleds and went to the mountain. We trudged through waist-deep snow and kept our heads above ground by clinging to tree trunks. By the end of winter we had selected the perfect building site. Sometime before spring the actress began making excuses not to go on our family outings, preferring the social activity of town. Nagging thoughts of another adolescent stuck on a farm twenty years before began to creep in.

The highlight of the spring season was showing our new property to Ace's parents who came to visit from Oklahoma. I should say "attempting to show" as opposed to "showing". Even after the snowmelt, the Vega couldn't climb the last mile and a half of the hill. We finally chugged to a stop and said, "Well, it looks pretty much like this on up at the top of the hill." Ace's mother's arthritic condition prevented our trek to the summit.

Our first trip to the mountain after the spring thaw was memorable indeed. We had never seen our land without a five-foot snow cover. When we finally saw it, we were hard put to recognize our domain. The beautiful expanse of green and white had been replaced overnight by a vast wasteland of fallen lodgepole pines, underbrush and junk. The shapely trees now showed ten feet of spindly trunks and often leaned under their own weight. Let me tell you, it was not a pretty sight! We were discouraged but not defeated. The land clearing would require much more time and labor than we had anticipated. The groundbreaking had to be put off for awhile. We decided not to set a date to avoid further disappointment.

We made a major investment in a chain saw, four pairs of work gloves and two dozen red bandannas. Red bandannas were the current fad in the Rocky Mountains at that time. You either tied the bandanna around your forehead (hippie style) or you tied the bandanna around your neck (country style) or you tied the bandanna around the neck of your Irish setter or golden retriever (woodsman style). We used our red bandannas to wipe sweat and swat flies. It was a long, hot summer. I struggled to conjure up visions of Tara. Ace composed proverbs of his own. All are unprintable.

Each week-end we packed a picnic lunch, the chain saw, the movie camera, the St. Bernard and our red bandannas in the Vega and headed for the hills. We cleared brush, cut trees and picked rocks until we were bruised and torn. It was a happy time, despite the aching muscles and blistered hands. During the spring run-off we found that we had a creek on our property. The athlete located a fallen log which lay across the creek. The log became her own private spot to dream and plan. Along the creek was a meadow where hundreds of delicate, blue and white columbines danced in the mountain breeze. The spring columbines were soon replaced by the vivid red of summer's Indian paintbrush. Each week brought new discoveries. The actress found a huge rock formation on which to perform. Gradually, the building site took shape - just before the first dusting of snow in August.

The highlight of our summer came quite by happenstance. Each week Ace reported our progress (or lack of) to his co-workers. They were all aware of our many trials and tribulations. During his weekly account, a fellow worker told Ace of a different type of builder out of Longmont, Colorado. He specialized in custom-built log homes. The homes were designed, cut to order and assembled at a Montana log lot. The logs were then numbered, disassembled and trucked to Colorado to be put together like Lincoln logs on the owner's land. It sounded like the house of our dreams! At $14 a square foot for the log shell, it was affordable. Our spirits were high as we trekked to Longmont.

The builder's home was the most beautiful thing I had ever seen. The mellow warmth of the massive, pine log walls and open beams was the most welcoming sight you can imagine. A fire in the substantial moss rock fireplace flickered and seemed to speak to my very soul. Spread out along the foothills, the house bore a striking resemblance to the Cartwright family ranch on "Bonanza". Ace and I fell in love with it on sight. While we couldn't afford anything so grandiose, our spirits soared at the idea of a simple log cabin instead of a kit house. The rustic warmth of the logs spoke of hardy self-sufficiency, grit and determination - all the qualities of life that we had found on our mountain. We drove back to Denver in high spirits to select a plan for our own real log, mountain home. And so I began a love affair which would last a lifetime - an affair with a log cabin.

Chapter 3

THE PLAN

I recalled other log cabins at other times and places in my life - the rustic Ozark Mountain cabins in Arkansas, the weathered, gray log cabin that sheltered George Washington at Valley Forge and the bloodstained floors of the Revolutionary War cabins along the New Jersey shore. I wanted a design that would speak as eloquently to future generations as those cabins had spoken to me. I pictured a log cabin nestled among the pines that would withstand years of Rocky Mountain snowfalls while comfortably serving the needs of our family.

Today's log homes are a far cry from the rude dwellings of America's pioneers. They combine early day craftsmanship with modern engineering to produce a home that offers the best of both. Builders' methods and styles are as varied as the houses themselves. They may be handcrafted or prepackaged, in full or half-log construction. In half-log homes the flat side of the logs is fastened to 2X4 or 2X6 stud walls. Interior walls may be drywall, paneling or half logs. The log home we selected was a handcrafted, full log package.

The first decision we had to make was the type of logs that would be used for the walls, the profile in which the logs would be fitted together and the style of the corner junctions. No single wood species stands out as being superior and there are no perfect logs. Log home builders utilize a variety of logs; pine, fir, red cedar, spruce or oak. Some home owners appreciate logs with character. They feel the lineal cracks (called "checks") or knots add to the rustic appeal. Other owners prefer a more contemporary, finished look and regard the checks as defects. I had mixed feelings. I loved the knots, but disliked the checks.

Handcrafted log builders rely upon several methods of log construction. Three of the most popular methods are the Scandinavian full-scribe, dovetail and round log chinked. In the Scandinavian style, the underside of each wall log is shaped to conform to the contours of the log beneath it. The dovetail style has the logs flattened on two sides with chink joints between the courses and dovetail corners. The round log chinked style (which we selected) used full round logs, with space between the courses of logs for the chinking. The logs were joined in saddle-notched corners. This was the junction style our builder preferred to use. Our logs were Ponderosa pine that had been fire-killed in Montana.

We were given the option of a custom design or a standard plan with some customizing of the features. Since standard plans were less expensive, we selected one of those. The maximum length of the logs determined the overall outside dimensions of the house. The inside log wall partitions could be adjusted to suit our needs.

We loved the look of the full log walls and planned

to keep the use of rough cedar to a bare minimum, using it only on closets and bathroom walls. We were limited to a forty foot exterior length. We selected a plan with a twenty-four foot exterior width. We wanted three bedrooms, a living room, combined kitchen/dining room and at least one bathroom. We looked upward to find the space we needed. One of the standard builder's plans included two loft-bedrooms built at opposite ends of the house and connected by a catwalk across the vaulted living room. The staircase could be crafted from individual logs or framed in. We selected full logs for the stairs and railings, with a framed floor for the catwalk. The plan looked very nearly perfect for our needs.

We planned to put the house on a full, walk-out basement to provide room for future expansion and a second bathroom. As the foundation was set into the side of the mountain, the walk-out basement would have an abundance of windows on one side. With a wrap-around deck on two sides of the house, we hoped to have a magnificent view of the Rockies to the west. The open floor plan of the big, country kitchen/dining room suited our lifestyle as well. I could picture our first Thanksgiving there, with Ace carving the turkey while I looked the part of the pioneer wife in my long, muslin apron. It was one of those moments when the anticipation far outweighs the reality.

One of the problems that comes with the territory of an owner-contracted house is bank financing. Bankers are hesitant to lend money on owner-constructed houses, especially log houses. We located a bank which offered a one-year construction loan while the house was being built. If the house met the bank construction requirements at the end of the year, it would then be refinanced with a conventional loan. The only requirement was that our building lot be fully paid for and used as collateral. We struggled to pay off the balance of our land. While the $14 a square foot price tag was reasonable for the shell, the builder told us that the finished house would cost approximately double that amount - even though we did considerable work ourselves. (That same log home builder's price today is $40 a square foot for the log shell.) In addition to the $28 a square foot finished price, we had to drill a well, install a septic tank and drainfield, dig a basement and pour the concrete footings.   I remembered one of Mother's quotes, "Where there's a will, there's a way", and learned to juggle bills with the best of them.

We laid out our past, present and future to the banker and waited. The construction loan was approved and we sent our design to the log lot in Montana. It was autumn.   The quaking aspens were golden on our mountain. It would be a struggle to pour the concrete footings before the winter freeze. Since we were building in the Rocky Mountains, we realized that hitting rock was a possibility, both in well-drilling and in digging the basement and drainfield. We contracted a geologist to take soil samples to determine the best location to dig and drill. A water witch with a divining rod could not have done worse. We hit rock formations a few feet down and had to blast for both the drainfield and the basement. I saw my carpet budget go up in dynamite blasting caps. The well-driller also hit solid rock and was forced to drill much deeper than he had anticipated. The well cost approximately twice the amount we had budgeted.

With construction well under way, we made more frequent trips to the mountain. The tired Vega stopped farther down the mountain with each trip. Our trek to the top seemed steeper each time. We could no longer postpone the purchase of a proper mountain car. It was a proud day when we were able to ride all the way to the top of the mountain in our new, red and white, 4-wheel drive International Scout. The Scout served us well, as there was room for the rest of us alongside Aspen and the ever present chainsaw.

Several weeks into the log lot operation the Longmont builder told us he had located a local engineer to erect the log shell on our lot. Because of logistics, the distance from Longmont and the tight time frame, he felt this would work well for all of us. The engineer was in the process of erecting his own log home - the first one he was to build. We were given his name and a local phone number. We made an appointment to meet him at his home.

The engineer and his family were living in a rented apartment while their log home was being built. Since he was struggling to build his own home before winter set in, he was reluctant to commit to building ours. In the course of the conversation we learned that his home was located on the same mountain that ours was. It seemed an incredible coincidence.

The next few weeks were tense. Our logs were ready for delivery and we had yet to get a firm commitment from the local engineer to erect the shell. First he said he would, then he said he wouldn't. Finally, the Longmont builder said he would do it by camping on the site for a few weeks. We breathed a sigh of relief.

The logs arrived in October, but not before the heavy snowfall. The logger's loaded truck had as much luck getting up that slippery mountain as our Vega. He finally gave up. We first saw our new log home at the foot of the mountain, stacked on a truck, with snow piling higher and higher.

The builder located a smaller logging truck, fitted it with a winch and took the logs up the hill - six logs at a time. It was an agonizingly slow process. At the site, each log was set in place with the winch. The logs were joined at the corners with ten-inch spikes. The sound of heavy mallets driving the spikes echoed down the snowy mountainside. The falling snow made the winter scene almost reverent.

After the first courses of logs were set in place, I stopped at the engineer's house to see how he was progressing. I had not yet forgiven him the time he had cost us while making a decision not to erect our shell. I found the engineer smoking his pipe, looking the picture of the hardy woodsman in his logger's cap, woolen pants and red suspenders. He was fighting the same winter weather that we were. It was hard to bear a grudge. As I stepped along the frozen ground looking at his house, something seemed vaguely familiar. All at once it hit me - the startling realization that I was seeing our log cabin in duplicate. Here was a log house exactly like ours on the same mountain! I was heartsick.

There was no turning back. Our only choice was to work with what we had. Ace and I were determined that our home would look different than the engineer's. Since our builder was as perturbed with him as we were, he was determined that our house would look better. He gave us a break on the price of the wrap-around deck, including a fully covered porch overhang and a wider deck than the engineer's. I wavered between avoiding the route up the mountain past the "other" house and being drawn there to see what it looked like. It was always a few weeks ahead of ours in construction.

Peter's Principle came into play at every turn. The builder and his crew were not accustomed to camping above 8,000 feet on a snow-covered mountain. They had the flu for more than a week. About the time they recuperated from the flu, one of the men slipped on the icy beams. He fell from the roof and broke his leg. Anything that could go wrong did go wrong. Since we were six months into our construction loan, time was of the essence. Finally, the shell was closed in, the cedar shake-shingled roof was on and windows and doors were in place. The house could withstand the winter.

While we were impatient with the winter weather, there was much to be done. The electrical contractor was able to wire the house. In full log homes all the wiring is done in conduit. Most of the conduit was concealed between the logs, behind the chinking or along the ceiling beams. Where overhead light fixtures were to be hung, the electrician drilled channels through the logs and threaded the conduit in the channels. By using electric baseboard heat, we avoided the ductwork of heating vents. Since conduit wiring is a tedious and time-consuming process, wiring a log home is usually more expensive than a comparable frame house.

Once the wiring was completed we were able to work in the house by using portable, electric heaters. The bathroom was the next room we tackled. It was an area where we utilized rough cedar walls to conceal plumbing pipes. We also used cedar for closets and storage cabinets. The rough cedar blended well with the log walls. Since we had only contracted for the log shell, most of the cedar walls were constructed by Ace. We made an investment in a skill saw to scribe the curvature of the logs. Ace was able to utilize his mathematical expertise in the calculations. I thought it would be simpler to use various sizes of plates, bowls and saucers to make a cardboard pattern, however I deferred to his judgement. Wise women know when to defer. My judgement calls regarding deferment were based on the noise level of the current proverbs and the color of the descriptive adjectives.

An area where Ace outdid himself was the curve of the stairwell framework beside a door leading to the basement. In the area where a cedar wall joined a log wall, it was necessary to exactly copy the curvature of the logs to fit the cedar wall. It was a tricky situation at best. Ace wisely postponed it until he had practiced several curves in less obvious places.

The door itself was a work of art, handcrafted from tongue and groove pine. Store bought, hollow core doors didn't blend with the scheme of things. Ace diligently handcrafted all our interior doors. They were a full winter's project. His education on the roll-top desk served him well.

With the temperature hovering near zero, we were anxious to close off the basement to conserve heat. The beautifully curved, cedar framework of the door was fitted to the logs before they had time to settle properly. It didn't take long for the logs to begin to settle. When they settled, the beautiful curves were in odd places. They were falling out all over the place - bursting forward where they should have receded, receding where they needed to burst forward. Like an overly endowed figure in a too small bikini, you wanted to push them back to where they belonged. Since these particular curves had several tons of logs resting on them, they were allowed to fall wherever they liked. Live and learn, I always say.

The fireplace was our next project. Since log homes are built with massive logs (and often have a vaulted ceiling), it is important to balance the logs with a massive brick or stone fireplace. Ace and I wanted a full wall of fireplace. We selected used brick for the construction. The brick fireplace wall went from the floor to the ceiling. It included a built-in woodbin and a raised hearth. It fit the personality of the house and provided an alternate heating system in case of a power outage. The fireplace chimney extended down to the basement where a woodstove would provide a heat source for the basement. Our primary heat source throughout the house was electric baseboard heat.

Log houses are remarkably energy efficient. Even though the logs don't have a particularly high R-value (a measure of heat resistance), the logs store heat during the day and release it slowly at night. As long as the logs aren't allowed to become totally cold, the house can be heated to a comfortable temperature in a short amount of time. Half-log houses actually have a higher R-value than full log houses do. Since our log house was at an altitude over 8,000 feet (and was surrounded by pine trees), heat was a primary consideration.

We designed the house to be as energy efficient as possible. This included a false roof above the vaulted ceiling, a full twelve inches of insulation and the roof of the house above that. Our vaulted ceiling had a rather interesting design not usually found on ceilings. At some point during construction, a worker stepped on a pine board which later became part of the ceiling. His bootprint remained visible after the board became the ceiling. As the telltale print was at an angle near the fireplace, I passed it off as Santa Clause making a hasty exit. The actress and the athlete were easily convinced. They hung their stockings each Christmas until they married.

While I loved the massive look of log walls, the thing I most admired in log houses was the chinking. Something about the simple efficiency of dried mud filling the cracks appealed to my primitive side. The space between the logs would be insulated with fiberglass batting strips before the chinking was applied. The chinking mud is added only after the logs have settled, to avoid cracking. While the backside of each log was grooved (the builder's term was "checked") with a chainsaw to control the natural twisting during the settling process, the additional settling time made for a tighter house. Some log builders leave the erected shell to settle as much as a year before adding the chinking. Since we couldn't mix the chinking mud in cold weather, our house was left to settle until spring.

The settling process occurs in all types of houses; be it brick, frame or log. That's why windows in old homes stick or doors are hard to open. A log home is more likely to settle (and will settle quicker) than a frame house. The reason for the settling is that logs standing in the forest are full of water. As soon as they are cut, the moisture begins to escape. Eventually, the log will reach a point of equilibrium with its environment. At that point the moisture content of the logs is equal to the moisture content of the surrounding atmosphere. When this happens, the logs shrink in circumference. While this shrinkage may be small for an individual log, when it is multiplied by the number of logs in the wall, it can account for one or two inches of space. That amount of space can make a critical difference in many areas. The beautiful curves along our cedar stairwell framework was a perfect example of what happens when a log house settles.

The length of settling time varies according to the type of logs used. Builders use a variety of types of logs; kiln-dried, air-dried, standing dead and green. Our fire-killed logs were of the "standing dead" variety. As a general rule, green logs will settle the most. Terms like "kiln-dried" or "standing dead" should not be regarded as magic words to solve the problem. Our "standing dead" logs shrank a good two to three inches overall.

Our first inkling that we were amateurs in the blueprint game concerned our layout of the interior walls. I wanted a big, country kitchen. We moved the living room wall to allow an extra foot in the kitchen. It was a case of robbing Peter to pay Paul. We did it without taking into consideration that the log staircase and the fireplace in the living room were fairly massive. By the time the staircase and fireplace took their share out of the living room, it appeared a bit out of proportion. It was narrow and dark. It somewhat resembled a large closet. At least Ace wouldn't have a glare on the television set when he watched the Sunday afternoon football games.

One of our major disappointments was due to our determination to make our house different than the "other" house. To preserve and finish the logs, a stain or wood preservative is applied to the finished shell, both interior and exterior. We had the option of selected a pre-mixed oil stain or concocting our own, using a linseed oil base. The other house was finished in a mellow, golden pine color. We mixed an original treatment - just a shade different. Anyone who has ever selected a carpet from a six-inch square only to find it miraculously change colors when expanded to ten or twelve feet will know what I am talking about. Our honey-colored, warm shade of stain in the can became a cool, russet brown when sprayed on the log walls of the house. It looked quite rustic - a cold, dark shade of rustic. We hoped the Colorado sunshine would lighten it. It never did.

Since we hadn't done well with the color of the logs or the living room layout, we turned our attention to interior decoration. I knew I could brighten up anything with enough color, my collection of copper pots and several hundred yards of muslin curtains. We were anxious for our log shell to begin to resemble a place where one might live one day. Selection of the kitchen cabinets made that day appear closer. Ace and I were in agreement on the cabinetry. We selected pre-built cabinets in the same wood and color as our pine trestle dining room table.

Cabinet installation in a log house requires a good bit of preparation work before the cabinets can be hung. Since the cabinets require a flat wall surface for mounting, the logs were planed to conform to exact cabinet dimensions. A 2"x4" framework was then attached to the log wall to provide a solid base for anchoring the cabinets to the wall.

I selected white, porcelain knobs for cabinet pulls to lighten things up. For some reason, the little, white knobs never did lighten the massive, russet brown logs. Since the house had an abundance of windows, I lightened it up by letting the sunshine in. I sewed yards of white, Cape Cod curtains to frame the windows. The curtain ruffles reminded me of the crinoline petticoats of my high school years. Each little flounce lifted my spirits.

The abundance of windows in the house aided in heating as well as lighting it. Today's log homes are designed to be energy efficient by retaining as much sunlight as possible. The builder's term is "passive solar". It quite simply means that homes are designed with an abundance of windows to admit the sunlight. Sunlight is most intense on the southern exposure and least intense on the north, with east and west in between. The log walls, floors or fireplace walls (called "heat sinks") absorb the heat and release it slowly, thereby making the house more comfortable while cutting the fuel bill.

One of the most important changes in today's log home building techniques is a result of upgrades in the quality of windows available. Windows with energy efficient glazing (such as low-E glass and argon-gas fill) are available to block the radiant heat flow. While we used double-paned windows in our log house, they were not nearly as energy efficient as today's windows. For example, today's south-facing window can yield two to three times as much heat gain as heat loss. The use of walls of windows also lightens up the feel of a log house. Natural sunlight makes the home's interior feel more spacious, bright and appealing. Since log walls can soak up a large amount of light, attention should be paid to adequate wall and overhead lighting.

Ace and I were anxious to move to our new home. The actress and the athlete had been settling in where they were. The actress had climbed the social ladder until she was firmly entrenched with the "popular" crowd. The athlete had landed a position on the teams of her choice. A change in schools would mean they had to start the painful process all over.

We made some headway when we took them to the "other" house and they saw first hand what spacious bedrooms they would have up in the loft. The engineer's loft bedrooms were huge! Our daughters began to plan entire complexes within their rooms for sleeping, studying and various other activities. They had never been blessed with so much space to work with. Since there would be plenty of room for slumber parties with all their friends from Denver, they began looking forward to showing off their new quarters.

The day the catwalk was finished, the actress and the athlete anxiously climbed up to explore their own loft bedrooms. With a chorus of wails, their anticipation came to an abrupt halt. While they could stand upright in the middle four feet of their rooms, the slope of the roof drastically diminished the headroom at the outside wall to the point that to utilize that space, they had to lie in a prone position. We realized we should have added three courses of logs around the entire house. That was what the engineer had done to the "other" house. He hadn't bothered to relay that information to us. As my mother always said, "Too little, too late." I was running out of proverbs.

We came home from the mountain one day to find the actress locked in her bathroom. She refused to come out of the bathroom and she refused to move to the mountain. She was prepared to do whatever it took to stay where she was. The athlete talked her out of the bathroom, however the situation did not improve.

The athlete sided with the actress. Now it was two

against two. Ace and I were losing ground. We were into bribery in a big way. When the athlete discovered it worked for the actress, we had to deal with her as well. She was easily bought, she wanted a horse. Since she could not have a horse in our suburban neighborhood, she agreed to move to the mountains if we got a horse within the year. (A subsequent chapter will deal with horse ownership in the Colorado Rockies.)

Dealing with the actress required more time, patience and ingenuity. I am convinced that her ability to land the starring role in "The Mad Woman of Chaillot" during her senior year of high school was a direct result of her theatrics regarding our move to the mountain. She played it to the hilt, trying a new tact each week. Since her parents were worn down from construction work, we were obviously an easy mark. And so we spent our last spring in Denver - cajoling, bargaining and bribing our eldest to move to the mountain at the end of summer. It was another long, hot summer.

Chapter 4

CHICKEN WIRE AND CHIPBOARD

There is absolutely no doubt that neither Ace nor I were carpenters in a past life. We can only hope that we are never carpenters in a future life. We paid our dues during the summer of '76. We served an apprenticeship in many areas. Fortunately, most of the required tools of the trade were not overly sophisticated. At least we weren't in serious danger of losing our limbs or suffering permanent disfigurement from the wire cutters or staple gun. I hadn't yet learned to sleep well with two power saws in the basement.

It was the season to add the chinking between the logs, both inside and outside. Chinking the exterior was necessary to pass inspection and thus qualify for our long awaited loan approval. Chinking the interior was strictly a matter of aesthetics. Perhaps there are women who would not mind a log house with pink fiberglass insulation stripes on the interior. I didn't happen to be one of them.

The fiberglass insulation was a sticky situation - sticky to eyes, nose, hands and any other body parts it came in contact with. It was especially irritating when it found its way between skin and underwear. It came in large bats which we unrolled and cut into strips with scissors. Even though we worked with gloves, the fiberglass particles cut through our gloves and embedded in our fingers. Working as deftly as possible, we stuffed the insulation strips between the cracks in the logs. At the end of each day, we were covered with glass slivers.

To anchor the chinking concrete, we cut strips of chicken wire one inch wider than the insulation strips. We attached the chicken wire to the logs with a staple gun, stapling both top and bottom. While the daughters and I were quite capable of cutting and stuffing insulation strips, we had a hard time cutting chicken wire. Even though there were three of us, it was impossible for us to stay ahead of Ace and the staple gun. The entire family began reciting proverbs. I pretended not to hear.

Since we had blown our carpeting budget to bits with all the dynamite blasting, we were left with chipboard sub-flooring. We had visions of an oak plank kitchen floor, with carpeting on the rest of the house. In the meantime, I cursed the ugly chipboard floors about as often as I cursed the pink fiberglass insulation.

I had become a hardy, mountain woman even though we had not yet moved to the mountain. I eyed the 12' X 16' moss green carpet on our family room floor. It had made a New Jersey garden apartment seem more like home. I had become quite capable at wielding scissors and wire cutters. With the help of the actress and the athlete, I moved the furniture, rolled up the carpet, loaded it into our trusty Scout and headed for the hills. By nightfall we had cut and fitted it to our new living room. As Mother always said, "Beauty is in the eye of the beholder." Perhaps my eyesight was impaired by the fiberglass insulation slivers, but the carpet looked beautiful. We could move in to one room that wasn't covered with exposed chipboard.

The chinking operation was a real mess. Modern materials have made chinking today's log homes easy and efficient. Today's chinking material flows in easily and will expand or contract with the changing seasons. In 1976, it was rough and dirty. Our chinking mud was made "from scratch". We combined a mixture of concrete, builder's sand, perlite and water. The desired result was mortar that would flow neatly into the cracks and stay there. The proper consistency was the tricky bit. Either it was too thick and wouldn't flow or it was too thin and dribbled out the cracks and down the logs. Any number of variables such as weather, heat and humidity affected the mixing process. It was necessary to mix a small amount at a time, as the drying process began the moment it was mixed. We were constantly mixing and stirring. With both the interior and exterior cracks to chink, we could have made it a lifelong career for the four of us. As it was, it only seemed that way.

One of the things we learned early on in building our log cabin was that each and every Colorado acquaintance harbored the same dream of building their own log cabin. In terms of popularity, it was right up there with Coors beer and downhill skiing. Since the majority of them would never pursue their own dream, they were more than anxious to help us pursue ours.

We had more offers of volunteer labor than we knew what to do with. We would have been wise not to do anything with it. At the time, we did not look a gift horse in the mouth.

Our "Let's all help old Ace build his log cabin" parties first appeared during the chinking process. As if it wasn't enough of a mess already, we had five or six good buddies arrive with a keg or two of beer. Old Ace couldn't oversee all their work. He was kept busy with attempts to rescue half-drunk chinker/friends from swinging rope scaffolds at two stories off the ground. They resembled monkeys in a three-ring circus, swinging up there with mortar boards and trowels. A troop of well-trained, circus monkeys would have done better work. On the north side of our house the chinking turned out as thick as the logs. Fortunately, it was always so cold that not too many people ever ventured around to the north side of the house to see it. The "other" house had nice, neat little lines of chinking.

After the outside walls were chinked, the long awaited loan approval was complete. We could finally move into our new home. It was an exciting day, despite our weary bodies and aching muscles. We felt like hardy pioneers by the time we moved the last load to the top of the mountain.

It was late summer. The nights were crisp and cool. The night seemed black after years of living with city street lights. It was lit with a million stars. At the top of our mountain, they were so close you wanted to reach out and touch them. On the other side of the mountain, the lights of Denver were light years away.

Just breathing the pure, mountain air was reason enough for all our trials and tribulations.

While the rewards of building our own home seemed to outweigh the negative aspects, one of the negatives was that it never seemed like a new house. I remembered moving into our first home with the new house smell and everything bright and gleaming. We moved into a construction area on the mountain. We hadn't yet chinked the interior logs. Except for the living room, the floors were chipboard sub-flooring. Everything was covered with a layer of sawdust and fiberglass insulation particles. We stepped over tools and sawhorses to get to the bathroom. Our work never left us and we never got away from it. We worked on the house at night after long days of commuting to Denver, spending a full workday and fighting the traffic home again. The proverbs became more and more colorful.

While Ace and I agreed that good, clean mountain living was a better life for our offspring than Denver's "brown cloud", we had not convinced them. We continued to be held hostage by the actress who was to begin her sophomore year in high school. We promised unlimited telephone privileges, the use of our recently acquired Volkswagen bug and frequent trips to Denver. None of it worked. She bought a little homemade plaque that said, "Bloom where you are planted", and moped in her loft.

The athlete spent most of her waking hours on her log, so she was easier to deal with. She was ready to start eighth grade at a small, mountain junior high school. Her fall school wardrobe consisted of her hiking boots, five pairs of Levis and a down-filled ski jacket. She bought a pair of riding boots in anticipation of the horse.

Both daughters had a difficult time standing upright in their loft bedrooms. Ace and I decided the budget had to stretch to include carpeting for their floors. We felt that if the floor was more inviting, they wouldn't mind its close proximity. We went the whole nine yards and gave them free rein in carpet selection. Long shag was the current style. They selected the longest shag possible. The athlete chose a sunny, lemon yellow. The actress opted for a bright, emerald green. Ace and I tried hard not to flinch. We lied through our teeth that it was the most beautiful carpet we had ever seen.

Ace installed the carpet by himself. Lugging the heavy rolls of shag carpeting up the log stairs and across the catwalk was a job in itself. It was a labor of love. Ace stretched and tacked the carpet while he lay on his stomach reciting proverbs under the low roofline of the loft. The carpet improved the situation somewhat. Since it appeared that our daughters could be bought we installed a telephone, a stereo system and a cat in each bedroom.

The actress found yet another homemade, wooden plaque to express her sentiments. (Her loft bedroom was beginning to resemble a Burma Shave graveyard.)

"Life is hard by the yard,
by the inch it's a cinch."

(A crayon inch-worm emphasized the point.)

I was forever struggling to recall Mother's appropriate proverbs. Sometimes they fit, sometimes they didn't. Sometimes I was too tired to care.

Chapter 5

ROCKY MOUNTAIN HIGH

During the months following our move to the high country, our delicate daughters were transformed into a construction crew with a surly attitude. Ace and I decided to try a new tact in mountain attitude adjustment. We would teach our daughters to love the mountains through recreation. While living in New Jersey, we invested in camping gear that never got used. The gear consisted of two small tents, four brown canvas sleeping bags with red-plaid flannel linings, a set of aluminum cooking utensils (complete with tin plates and plastic cups) and a Coleman four-burner stove. The actress and the athlete called us "the Coleman family".

It never occurred to us that our gear might not be entirely suitable for camping in the Rocky Mountains. The reason that it never occurred to us was that it was the middle of July. Both Ace and I had grown up in Oklahoma. One does not consider the possibility of being cold in the middle of summer after growing up in Oklahoma.

We packed the Coleman gear, the offspring and Aspen in the Scout and headed for the high country.

Since we lifted off at 8,000 feet and spent a good half day driving straight up, I will not venture a guess at the altitude where we landed. It was a magnificent day! We were surprised that the north side of the mountains had a few inches of snow accumulation. We found the perfect campsite beside a stream we assumed to be full of trout. While there was a slight slope to our campsite, we reasoned that living on a mountainside should compensate for the slope. We pitched our tents and got to the serious business of fishing. The athlete landed a six-inch brookie. The rest of us didn't fare so well. We had packed plenty of food, so this was not a problem. We cooked our supper over the campfire, roasted marshmallows and used them as torches to warm our hands.

It had been a long day. We decided to turn in early. The woods were dark and scary. The daughters thought there should be one parent in each tent. The athlete and I got the site with the steepest slope. Ace, the actress and Aspen took the one with the most rocks. It seemed like a fair trade. We curled up in our sleeping bags and talked about what fun we were having. We tried hard to be convinced. We fell asleep listening to the strange night sounds.

Sometime during the night, the slight incline we had gone to bed with began to elevate itself. The athlete and I slid down the hill and landed in a heap at the front of the tent. The interior of the tent was stone cold. We were not about to venture out of the sleeping bags to rearrange ourselves. On the count of three, we bounced our way back to the top of the hill. By the time the count reached five, we slid back to the bottom. Up and down, up and down. We picked up the tempo each time we did it. Finally, at about three in the morning we gave it up. We settled for the down position. I lay awake - tired, sore and cold. I tried hard to think of a suitable proverb to lift my spirit.

"Cold hands, warm heart."
(Not exactly what I had in mind.)

"It's always darkest just before the dawn."
(Still cold. Think warm.)

"Out of the frying pan, into the fire."
(My life's story. Still cold.)

Much to my surprise, I fell asleep and stayed asleep until sunrise. Ace had built a fire and made coffee by the time I crawled out of the tent. I would have a hot breakfast sizzling on the tin plates when the daughters awoke. There's just nothing like a hearty breakfast of bacon and eggs to start the day off right. The athlete had ordered her trout for breakfast. It would fry along with the bacon. The hearty aroma of bacon frying drifted through our campsite. Within minutes it was on the tin plates. Within two seconds the bacon grease froze solid, same with the trout. Ditto with the eggs. As I always say, there's just nothing like a good, hot cup of coffee to start the day out right.

Living with wildlife in the mountains was a new experience for us. Aspen alerted us to any new arrivals. She spent her days barking at chipmunks, birds and squirrels. The chipmunks could be found picking the fiberglass insulation from around the basement foundation, making their own winter preparations. I had visions of our entire mountain overrun by itching, scratching chipmunks after hibernation with the glass slivers. The squirrels were always scavenging from the bird feeders. Aspen was kept busy with her guard duties.

Very early one morning, she barked frantically before making a mad dash through the kitchen door. Doors were still only a minor inconvenience to Aspen. I never saw the door she couldn't open. I assumed that whatever sent her through the door must be bigger than a squirrel. Through the open door, I saw a most unexpected sight. An elk herd was making its way across our yard. I had never seen more than a few elk and then only at a great distance. I woke the family to experience the sight. We were surrounded by at least a hundred elk. It was one of our more memorable wildlife moments.

The actress had an exciting adventure with the resident wildlife our first summer. She had taken to sunbathing on our deck. Either modesty or stylishness deemed it necessary that she carry a pair of cut-off jeans to wear over her bathing suit at appropriate times. She left the cut-offs laying on the deck when she wasn't wearing them.

After one sun-bathing session, she pulled on the cut-offs and went to her room to read. After half an hour of reading, the actress began dancing and screaming. I supposed she was trying a new tact in her attempt to get back to Denver. It was original. I had to give her credit for that. She finally stopped the war dance, deciding I was not impressed. The actress ripped off the cut-offs and launched into another tirade. It was one of her more memorable lifetime performances.

Apparently, a chipmunk had crawled into her pocket while the jeans were on the deck. After peacefully sleeping in the pocket while she read, it woke up and began to squirm. That's when the performance began. After the rude awakening, the chipmunk hobbled off a little the worse for wear. The athlete had to hunt him down and help him out the door.

On occasion the younger daughter could also become quite dramatic. She was prone to soaking in the bathtub. We heard her screaming during one of her leisurely soaks. We assumed she was either close to drowning or had discovered a zit on her nose. We went to the door to investigate, in case it was the former. She hastily grabbed her robe and was hopping wildly about the bathroom. She was screaming, "Somebody get this *!#* squirrel out of my bathtub!"

By that time, a half-drowned squirrel had managed to get its own self out of the bathtub. It was also hopping wildly about the bathroom. The athlete gave a performance equal to her sister's chipmunk melodrama.

After the frightened squirrel was set free and the athlete calmed down to the point of mild hysteria, we pieced together the series of events. The athlete first took note of the squirrel as she heard splashing sounds from the toilet. Apparently, the squirrel came down an outside vent pipe and found its way up through the toilet bowl. It then leaped from the toilet to the bathtub, thus creating all the fuss from the occupant in the tub. We added another lesson in mountain home building. Always cover bathroom vent pipes with steel mesh squirrel baffles.

At times we were plagued with other mountain visitors. With Aspen making frequent grand entrances through the kitchen door, it was often left standing wide open. Various forms of wildlife wandered in. I have spent many an hour chasing down chipmunks that were scavenging for better insulation. On several occasions, bats flew in the open door. Since bats in the Rocky Mountains are known to carry several diseases, capturing the bats was a tricky procedure. Our vaulted living room ceiling was the perfect bat escape tunnel. The athlete developed a powerful tennis swing while sitting astride the catwalk railing. Her tennis racquet was our standard bat weapon of choice. We eventually trained the family cats to be excellent batters.

After growing up in the country (with a summer bounty from the garden), I figured now that we were country folk, we should have our own garden. Ace cleared a spot right out front where our garden would be convenient to show off to our neighbors when they stopped by. He rented a garden tiller and plowed up a good-sized garden patch. Ace lined up the little rows as only a skilled mathematician could. He plotted our entire garden patch out on graph paper, so as to allow room for the beans to climb, the corn to pollinate and the squash to wander. I bought little onion sets and seed packets early in the spring, so we'd be ready at the last frost. Since the last frost didn't come till late June, we would have a late garden. In Oklahoma, sometimes my grandad planted a late garden and was still harvesting garden sass (Grandad's term for produce) at Thanksgiving.

The whole family helped plant our garden in late June. We were proud when it was all patted down and in the ground. The green tops of the little onion sets made it look like a real garden. We watched for the lettuce and radishes to peek through the soil. Since the nights were still in the thirty degree range, it took a little longer for the seeds to sprout than we anticipated. The onions didn't take off growing as fast as they usually did in Oklahoma. Sometime after the Fourth of July, the lettuce finally peeked through. The radishes followed shortly after. We weeded and watered and contemplated fertilizer to speed things along.

By the first of August, the appearance of the onion sets hadn't changed a whole lot. We harvested a leaf or two of lettuce, but the radishes hadn't yet begun to make radishes. The beans, corn or squash never did make an appearance. When the neighbors stopped by, we reckoned that the rabbits were eating the garden as fast as it came up. They sympathized. When the first snowfall came on August nineteenth, we stopped watering and weeding. We figured we'd start earlier the following spring.

We heard there were ripe chokecherries in Deer Creek Canyon, so our attention turned to putting up jam and jelly. While we picked chokecherries, we found a bounty of brilliant red, rose hips. We came home with picking baskets full of both. We felt like hardy, self-sufficient mountain folk as we sorted the stems from the chokecherries and laid the rose hips out to dry. We simmered and ladled the chokecherry juice into cute jelly jars embossed with fruit designs. For some reason, the jelly never did jell. We called it Mountain Chokecherry syrup and served it on pancakes.

Our mountain rose hip tea was another matter entirely. We mixed the dried rose hips with fragrant spices of cinnamon, cloves and dried orange peel. We packaged it in jars with red, gingham ties around the lids. The rose hip tea we brewed was amber colored and brisk. It was so brisk it seemed alive. The rose hip tea was alive! It began to crawl. A kindly neighbor told us we should have waited to harvest the rose hips until after the frost, in order to kill the bugs.

Mountain cooking was an education all in itself. In my previous, low-altitude life, I just assumed the high-altitude instructions on cake mix boxes were put there to fill up space. It was cheaper for Betty Crocker to put high-altitude directions than coupons on the side of her boxes. I never paid much attention to them in Denver and couldn't tell much difference in the results.

My first experience with high-altitude cooking over 8,000 feet was a pot of dried, pinto beans. Being a woman with a Southern upbringing, I loved pinto beans and cornbread. I loved the smell of ham hocks simmering for hours and the look of golden corn muffins in the iron muffin pan. It was one of those earthy times when you felt that all was right with the world, getting back to basics like that. It seemed like an appropriate meal up at the top of the mountain in Spindly Pines.

I sorted the rocks from the pinto beans and put them to soak the night before. The next day I added a couple of good-sized, smoked ham hocks and put the beans to simmer. Mother taught me to add a pinch of soda to the beans, so as to alleviate some of the gas early on. I tossed in the soda. You can't believe what a little pinch of soda can do at an altitude over 8,000 feet. The pot liquor began to froth and foam like those ham hocks were alive. It foamed right over the top of the pan and made a steaming, boiling mess on my brand new stove. I cleaned up the mess and turned the heat down, figuring I'd learned my lesson about high altitude cooking.

I simmered those pinto beans all day long. At supper time they were still hard little rocks. They had a good crunch when you tried to sink your teeth in them. I'd never had pinto beans quite like that before. As it turned out, the corn muffins were a little different as well. They rose so high, they escaped the iron muffin pan. Then they fell right back down. They were short, squatty little corn muffins with the golden brown crust left on the rim of the iron muffin pan. It was a much earthier meal than I'd ever had the pleasure of eating.

That first year almost every meal was a lesson in high altitude cooking. Miss Scarlett's plantation recipes were not easily adapted to mountain cooking. In one holiday season alone, there was the angel food cake lesson, the praline candy lesson and the pecan pie lesson. That was one of the worst messes I ever scraped off an oven floor. After a time, any cooking failure was blamed on the altitude. Ace learned to live with it. The actress and the athlete developed a taste for salads.

And so we spent our first year on our mountain - sometimes happy and sometimes sad - working and playing at being hardy mountain folk. Sometimes it was hard to tell where one emotion stopped and the other started, or where play became work or work became play. It was a fine line. We never knew when we crossed it.

Chapter 6

SPINDLY PINES

Nestled among the foothills to the west of Denver, you will find any number of mountain communities. Most of them are planned developments with entrance pillars of moss rock or rustic, split-rail fences and picturesque names. They are laid out by developers who know what they are doing and are as well planned as any Denver metropolitan sub-division. Water lines, sewer pipes and streets are installed before a single house is built. Wiring is often underground and building codes restrict all homes to conform to an aesthetically pleasing color scheme. This didn't happen to be the case with our mountain.

Spindly Pines was a mountain sub-division that from all outward appearances had been neither planned nor well thought out. About the only element of the aforementioned schedule of activities was that a road had been slashed out amongst the trees. It seemed to take the path of least resistance and wound in a spiral from the bottom up to the top of the mountain. It had three or four hairpin curves and several switchbacks. It was rough and rocky when it wasn't covered with ice and snow. Then it was slippery, rough and rocky. You had to be a hardy soul to want to traverse that road.

Because of the road being laid out first, the lots were in various shapes and sizes, none of which were square. Some were pie-shaped, some resembled a hexagon, many were strange shaped with a triangle on one side and a square on the other. An aerial view of Spindly Pines sub-division would have proved interesting indeed. Most of the lots were at least five acres, which was about the only desirable aspect of owning one of them. At least you didn't have neighbors within your adjoining five feet of rocky slope. That was most likely a good thing. Taking into consideration the unique type of hill person that usually settled in Spindly Pines and the unique configuration of the lot divisions, there would most certainly have been some property line feuds of a serious nature.

Most of the picturesque sub-divisions were inhabited by professional people. They were a mix of doctors, lawyers and corporate executives seeking a pastoral kind of life. They were bland communities totally lacking in local color. That was not the case with Spindly Pines. Our mountain had more local color than some people could tolerate. Since our neighbors kept pretty much to themselves, it took awhile to get a handle on their mountain lifestyle. It was probably better that way. I don't know that I could have handled life on the mountain in one big dose all at once.

Before I introduce you to our neighbors, let me tell you that all their names have been changed to protect their privacy. These were rugged, hard-working people who had managed to escape the confines of the city. It was not an easy life and the mountain had tempered them. After a few years of living there, they mellowed into real mountain folk. While you respected their privacy, you always knew the neighbors were there if you needed them. I never had a problem that at least one person on the mountain didn't know how to deal with it. They were good-hearted, generous mountain people. I imagine they were very much like my hill country ancestors in North Carolina.

At the foot of the mountain set the original homestead. At least it appeared to have been there several years longer than any of the other mountain homes. That assumption is based on the fact that several additions appeared to have been added on at ten year intervals. The original dwelling looked to have been a two-room shack with a tin roof and tar paper siding. The chicken pen was attached to that, where seven or eight white leghorn hens were usually kept. Being a farm kid, I knew for a fact that those hens would never lay an egg because of the cold Colorado winters. I figured they were being fattened for Sunday dinners.

The next addition to the house featured fake red-brick siding and a green composition roof. The roof was two shades of green. Apparently, they found a bargain on roofing at two different times. The windows in that addition were shorter and more abundant. They were filled with house plants and had bright, red-checkered curtains. It appeared to be the kitchen.

The next addition was quite large and added at a sharp right angle to the rest of the house. It was built from used lumber scavenged from various places. Some of the lumber was plywood sheets which at first looked temporary.　After five years you figured they were probably permanent.

Besides the houseplants in the window, there were several galvanized tin washtubs of red petunias in the yard to brighten up the place.　There was also a white toilet bowl in the yard.　The first two years I assumed they were in the process of installing indoor plumbing. The third year it was filled with red petunias.　I never did decide if that was its intended purpose all along.

The yard was filled with a lifetime of junk cars, cast off when they no longer served their purpose.　They were in various stages of rusty abandonment.　The teenaged mechanic who lived there always had the hood up on one or two of the cars, attempting to combine their parts into one functional vehicle.　His only reliable transportation was a snowmobile which sat there summer and winter.　Since the only month that it didn't snow on the mountain was in July, that was just as well.　It was the only snowmobile on the mountain. During the winter months the mechanic was quite popular.

During the fall, the mechanic was a tackle on the high school football team.　The hefty lineman came uncomfortably close to decking Ace at a local bar one night.　The actress had accompanied the football player and a group of friends to the game room adjoining the bar for a game of pool.　Upon seeing his daughter, Ace wandered over.　He put his arm around her shoulder and said, "Hello, Babe, what are you doing here?" (Ace was prone to using pet names for all of us.)　He had never met the football player close up.　The lineman

68

didn't appreciate his date being called "Babe" by a man old enough to be her father. The actress managed the introduction just in the nick of time.

A bit further up the hill was the Schnafner clan. They were a large family with eight or ten white-haired boys. They appeared to range from five to eighteen years of age. Mrs. Schnafner was a wild-haired, mountain woman. In previous years, she had been too busy raising the boys to learn to drive. Since all of her sons drove (including the ones who couldn't see over the steering wheel), she decided it was time to learn to drive. The Spindly Pines road was not the best place to get your driver's learning permit. Once Mrs. Schnafner got hers it was definitely not a road you drove by choice.

Many was the time we were forced to take to the ditch when we met the wild-haired woman in her old Jeep truck as she blasted up the mountain. Being a little apprehensive about driving, she took the position that the faster she drove, the sooner her ordeal was over. She rammed the accelerator to the floor and blasted off up the hill - always seeking the middle of the road. You only hoped that you met her when you were on the side of the road next to the mountain. There were no guardrails on the opposite side. Since the pine trees didn't appear sturdy enough to stop a rolling car, it would have been a long, rough roll down the mountain to Denver.

Just past the Schnafner's place was the property of John Brown, our most notable mountain resident. John was a Denver Bronco football player. He didn't live in Spindly Pines fulltime. It was his mountain getaway.

He entertained friends and stabled his expensive, chestnut thoroughbred horse there.

Being a benevolent sort of guy, John Brown tried to help the underprivileged boys of the inner city. He invited some of the boys up to his house to enjoy the mountains and ride the horse. They weren't much interested in mountains or horses, but they did find some interesting loot in the neighbor's house when they robbed him. John Brown abandoned his plan of benevolence early on in deference to the neighbor.

The thoroughbred horse was a thing of beauty. Each time our horse lover saw the elegant beast, she became more insistent about acquiring her own horse. Ace and I kept stalling. We didn't want to spoil her anticipation.

The engineer and his family moved to the mountain a few months before we did. They appeared to be the ideal, All-American family. The engineer was of German descent, sturdy and dark. His dark hair was prematurely graying, but his thick mustache above the ever present pipe was still black. He spoke quietly and deliberately, often lighting the pipe as he carefully chose his words.

His wife was a blonde, Nordic beauty. She was usually tanned from skiing, bright and bubbling with enthusiasm. Their son was two years younger than our youngest. Their daughter was two years younger than her brother. They seemed to be a close, fun-loving family. If we hadn't all been so busy commuting to Denver and working on the log houses, we would probably have become friends. As it was, we waved as we passed each other on the mountain.

Our nearest neighbors were the Olafsons. They were a hardy, Norwegian family of four who had not yet learned the ins and outs of life in America. The parents command of the English language was fairly fluent, but with a heavy Norwegian accent. The two teenage children were typically American. They were rapidly losing their Norwegian mother tongue. Since we were on the same four-party telephone line as the Olafsons for several months, our offspring became fairly fluent in colorful Norwegian proverbs.

The Olafsons didn't mind roughing it, which was a good thing. They hadn't been able to procure bank financing to build on their property and were living in a series of more or less temporary shelters. The first was an ancient Volkswagen van. They expanded the living quarters to include a lean-to shack and parked the van next to it. During the winter, they put a wood stove in the lean-to and seemed quite cozy.

Ole and Lena Olafson were both accomplished storytellers. They entertained many nights in exchange for their supper. The only problem was that after Ole had a few beers, he never went home. He stamped his cigarette butts on whatever carpet he happened to be on. This particular habit didn't set too well if you had a carpet. Since we entertained Ole on chipboard floors, it wasn't a problem.

For the most part the Olafsons seemed to thrive on their lifestyle. It bothered the neighbors more than it bothered them. We all worried about the Olafsons when the deep, winter snowfall came. They kept a herd of goats for milk and cheese and relied on a diet heavy on garlic to keep them healthy. They appeared to be in fine form. The garlic aroma always moved in well ahead of them. You always knew when there was an Olafson on your property.

One winter a soft-hearted neighbor with an empty house lent it to the Olafsons in return for caretaking. A magnificent, pine tree stood in the front yard. Such trees were rare in Spindly Pines. The beautiful tree was the property owner's pride and joy. The Olafsons had a cat which delighted in climbing the big, pine tree. One day Ole lost patience with the cat when it refused to come down from the tree. He took out his chainsaw and chopped the tree to the ground. Ole said he taught that #*!* cat a thing or two!

Dave and Ingrid Hill were one of the more unusual couples. Ingrid was an attractive, German woman and old enough to be Dave's mother. Dave was not much older than Ingrid's daughter who was also named Ingrid and lived with them. Dave and Ingrid Sr. had a young son of their own. Dave didn't have a regular job except for tending to John Brown's thoroughbred horse. He was a free spirit, doing odd jobs here and there. As our dinner table conversation often included the subject of horse ownership, it was good to have a horseman/handyman nearby.

The police chief of one of the affluent Denver suburbs lived on our mountain. We felt safe and protected knowing there was a squad car on our mountain. Even when the police chief was fighting crime in the city, his absence was comforting. We assumed that any would-be burglars would know there was a squad car on our mountain and seek their fortunes elsewhere.

On any Colorado mountain you will find a few eccentrics who simply chose to drop out of society. We had a few of those as well. Some were employed, some weren't. For one reason or another, they had a hard time living in the city. They each had a story. You rarely heard it.

One summer our mountain had its own nudist colony. The colonists were a group of airline flight attendants based in Denver. Cold weather hampered their activities. They disbanded after the first serious snowfall. Apparently, they were not a hardy strain of colonists.

The athlete encountered an entire band of free spirits camping on the abandoned roadbed which was our sledding hill. Actually, she watched them from afar - which was probably a good thing. They sat around a campfire most of the time, smoking pot and singing. They looked to be a cross between flower children and Jackpine savages. After awhile they moved on.

The one thing the residents of Spindly Pines had in common was that we all struggled. We struggled with the weather or we struggled with the business of making a living. Most of the time we struggled with both. All of us struggled with the trials and tribulations of building a house with a budget not quite as big as it called for.

Just about the time the struggle seemed overwhelming, the snow would melt and the columbines would bloom. The elk would come down from the high country and the mountain streams would flow. A Rocky Mountain high would pervade the mountain and all its inhabitants. That's the time we would look at the snowcapped peaks to the west and say, "It just doesn't get any better than this."

Chapter 7

SHAMROCK & NICKY

Life on the mountain seemed to get a little easier after our first year. Maybe we just learned to endure the hardships a little better. Maybe we were just too busy driving up and down Spindly Pines Drive to think about how hard it was.

Both Ace and I worked in Denver. I worked a split schedule, so we commuted separately. Both of our daughters learned to drive on the mountain. At one time our family owned three vehicles and still had to juggle transportation. The athlete played three sports. It was always one ball season or the other. The actress was involved in the high school drama club which met after school hours. We met ourselves coming and going.

Both daughters eventually settled into life on the mountain. It wasn't easy. The city boys didn't help matters any. The athlete was once told by a future attorney that he'd be happy to date her if she would chip in on the gas money. She was told more than once that a condition of a date was that she meet them at the foot of the mountain. She never did. She did make it a point to check out their access to a four-wheel drive vehicle. It was a similar situation that I had with the family hog trucks when I was her age. Our daughters learned early on that it could be a long, cold winter.

Both the actress and the athlete seemed to have an affinity for city boys - just as I had in my dating days. Maybe it's just that the grass always looks greener on the other side of the fence. The actress went so far as to bring a city boy home as a week-end house guest. Things were serious enough that she thought he ought to get to know her family better. Her first mistake was in bringing him in the winter. His city car never made it past the first switchback. His winter footwear was a pair of Reebok jogging shoes. By the time they hiked up the mountain in the knee-deep snowfall, the city boy had caught a cold. The actress coddled him all week-end with down comforters and chicken soup. The relationship seemed to flounder after that.

We gradually added all the comforts of home to our log cabin. Ace installed a beautiful, oak plank kitchen floor complete with wooden pegs. Installing the oak planks was not one of his easier jobs as the log supporting joists were not always uniform. Despite the many hours he spent planing the logs, the oak floor tended to roll in a few places. It was a homey, country kitchen. It looked exactly as I imagined it would and was my pride and joy.

The final touch to our home came the day the wall to wall carpeting was installed in the rest of the house. I wanted copper carpet while Ace had an affinity for blue. Luck was with us when we found a multi-colored copper and blue mix. We contracted for the carpet installation which made it a real luxury. The carpet was beautiful, however with the russet brown logs and narrow living room, it also changed colors once it left the store. It was darker by the time it was laid on the floor. As time passed, I stopped having nightmares featuring chipboard and pink fiberglass monsters. I haven't had one for at least five years.

With the addition of carpet to our home, Ace and I were running out of excuses not to build the horse corral. We always kept our promises to our daughters. This would be no exception. Ace got out the trusty chainsaw and we got back to clearing land for the corral. Since Ace was not a horse lover, his proverbs were usually muttered under his breath.

Being a farm kid, I knew a horse needs wide open spaces, a pasture to graze and a pond to drink from. We didn't happen to have any of those things. I figured we could make do with what we had. What we had was a rocky hill full of lodgepole pine trees. To make the best use of the materials at hand, Ace fashioned the corral from the lodgepole pines. He cleared a fairly wide circle for the corral and used the trees on the edge of the circle as posts. He trimmed the branches off the felled trees to make a rail fence and a gate for the corral. Four tiers of the rails nailed to the posts served as the fencing. It was a rustic sort of corral.

Ace left a few trees on the interior of the corral for scratching posts. On occasion in Oklahoma, we had seen docile farm animals backed up to scratching posts, rubbing an itchy flank. We didn't want to deprive our horse of a good scratching post.

Winters could be rough on our mountain. We wanted our horse to have adequate winter protection. Ace left trees at critical points to serve as the framework for a shed. He framed in the trees on three sides, covered the frame with a roof and added a feed trough at the rear. When he finished, it was a fine home for a horse.

At that time, Ace informed us that he had done his part. The remainder of the horse acquisition was up to the athlete and me. Since I was the parent who had promised the horse, from here on out I would be the one to deliver. I figured fair is fair and got to work on the rest of it. After all, I was the parent who was the farm kid and I should know about livestock. This didn't seem to be the time to admit that I hadn't gone near the horse barn since I was five years old.

Since we didn't have a farm pond in Spindly Pines, I located a galvanized aluminum watering tank. I figured a horse wouldn't drink more water than we could bucket down the hill. The athlete needed to stay in good physical shape for the sports she played. She would welcome the job of toting the water buckets. We were fortunate that the mountain village near us had a feed store where we could purchase hay bales and grain. It seemed a good omen that horses were indeed meant to live in the mountains.

Horse shopping didn't take long. The Denver Post Sunday classifieds had several horses listed for sale. I called the first ad. Fortunately, they still had the horse they advertised. The athlete and I drove down to the horsey Denver suburb to take a look. It was exactly what we pictured - a beautiful meadow full of grazing horses. The horse in question was a four-year old half quarter horse and half appaloosa, a handsome Irish steed named Shamrock. He was black with unusual white markings on his rump and sides. The owner assured us that Shamrock was well-trained. He asked if we would like to ride the horse. We said, "No, of course not." Our reluctance was due to the fact that the athlete had never ridden a horse. My riding experience was limited to sitting astride the farm plow horses as they ambled between the corn rows at crop gathering time. I was four years old at the time. This didn't seem to be the time to discuss our previous qualifications for riding a horse.

I did know about horsetrading. My daddy was an accomplished horsetrader. I knew for a fact that he never offered the asking price. The owner was asking $500 for Shamrock. I sauntered around the horse for a bit, praying that he didn't kick backwards. Very slowly (with what I deemed to be an appraising stance), I looked him up and down. I scrutinized a blemish or two, so as to appear more knowledgeable. While I knew Daddy always looked at an animal's teeth, I couldn't bring myself to open those thick, horsey lips to take a peek. After a suitable appraisal time, I made my offer. With my best poker face I said, "$475". The owner smiled broadly and exclaimed, "He's yours!"

We didn't own a horse trailer, but I knew I could rent one. I told the man we would pick Shamrock up the following day. Another thing I had never done on the farm was back a horse trailer. It never appeared to be overly difficult. My daddy and my brother backed trailers all over the farm. Since I was a farm kid, I figured I'd know how whenever the time came to back a horse trailer. Since it appeared that Ace intended to stick to his decision to turn the horse dealing over to me, I reserved a rental trailer.

The U-Haul agent hitched the horse trailer to the Scout and never even asked if I knew how to drive a trailer. He did seem a trifle concerned about adequate insurance coverage. I figured the "Adventure in Moving" motto on the side of the trailer was there for a reason. I climbed in the Scout and began the adventure.

I knew that driving a horse trailer down a mountain highway could be tricky. I tested the braking time as I descended Interstate 70. Not once was I forced to use the runaway truck escape ramps. It was clear sailing all the way to Denver. I felt like a real horsewoman as I trailered up to the pasture full of horses.

Loading Shamrock was not a problem. Apparently, he had gone this route before. His previous owner obviously knew how to handle him. I waved good-bye and remembered to pull the trailer slowly down the drive. Once I ascended the mountains, braking was not a problem. I was pulling up hill all the way. I had no intention of stopping on the way home. It was one of the smoothest trips up the mountain I ever made. The weight of Shamrock and the trailer made the washboards on Spindly Pines Drive level right out. I was proud as I pulled our horse down the driveway.

Ace worked late that day. I was not about to take

that horse out of the trailer without assistance. Shamrock was forced to spend his first night in the trailer. The next morning he was not overly happy. There was a wild look in his eyes as he stamped impatiently against the trailer gate. Ace bravely took on the job of leading Shamrock to the corral.

Shamrock didn't settle in easily. He ran faster and faster around the circle of the corral. He was obviously feeling a little hemmed in and missing the other horses. He stopped running only to eat and drink. We figured he would get used to his new surroundings in a day or two. In the meantime, we decided not to do any riding. I had plenty to do that day as it was, backing the horse trailer out of the driveway. I finally made it on the nineteenth try.

After a day of running the fence, the look in Shamrock's eyes was wilder than ever. His nostrils flared. Neither the athlete nor I tarried anywhere near the corral. We made a mad dash with the grain can and water bucket. We made an even hastier retreat. It was obvious that Shamrock was not settling in to mountain life.

The third day marked Shamrock's first escape. He sized up the strength of the lodgepole pines, made a run at them and kept on going. The corral was in shambles and Shamrock was nowhere to be seen. I had a hard time wanting to look for him. I remembered one of Mother's proverbs that fit the situation perfectly.

"Close the barn door after the horse is gone."

Still, in deference to the neighbors I felt a nagging sense of responsibility to locate the wild horse. I set off tracking his hoofprints with the bridle in hand. I found him in Dave Hill's horse corral, shyly nuzzling John Brown's thoroughbred. Docile as a lamb, he was only seeking companionship. At least he had good taste in companions.

With Dave Hill's help, I bridled Shamrock. Actually, Dave bridled Shamrock while I kept my distance as best I could without appearing to be obviously afraid of the horse. Dave admired the beautiful horse, jumped on his back and rode him around the corral bareback. He offered to ride him home. I tried not to accept too quickly.

The next day was a repeat of the previous one. Shamrock broke out of our corral and into Dave's. I dragged him home, none too gently. Indignant, Shamrock bit me on the arm. The doctor said I needed a tetanus shot. I reacted to the shot. Now I had a sore, swollen arm in various shades of black and blue and a wild, Irish horse that refused to stay at home.

It became a battle of wills. I would break that horse's cantankerous spirit or die trying. Each day I bridled and saddled Shamrock, rode him hard and put him away wet. After a few days, he seemed docile enough to trust with the athlete. She did a few walks around the yard and decided she was ready to ride. After all, she had five pairs of Levis, a cowboy hat and a pair of riding boots. She was seriously contemplating a western shirt. The actress was afraid her sister was becoming a hick.

During the ride, the athlete happened to squeeze her knees against Shamrock's belly. Until that moment, we had been unaware that Shamrock was trained to "knee rein". Dave Hill later explained to us that the tighter the athlete's knees pressed against the horse's belly, the faster Shamrock ran. The faster he ran, the tighter she squeezed. It was a vicious circle. They galloped at full speed around the mountain - the athlete hanging on for dear life and Shamrock running for the roses. The ride ended with the athlete refusing ever to mount that wild horse again. Dave Hill took pity on us and took him off our hands for $350. Some lessons are more expensive than others.

After the Shamrock lesson, both the athlete and I were savvy horse dealers. We started looking for a tamer steed. We asked around. We avoided the classifieds. It was the actress who got wind of a horse named Nicky. He belonged to a friend. Nicky was a small, gentle, sorrel gelding. He was older. We assumed he was wiser.

Nicky was a bargain. We gave the $250 asking price and didn't try to horsetrade. It didn't seem gracious to try to horsetrade with friends. Nicky was delivered, ridden up the mountain bareback by the friend. He seemed to enjoy his corral and his scratching posts. He backed right up to one and started rubbing his rump. It was exactly the way we pictured it. We were proud as we patted Nicky and he nuzzled our fingers.

Nicky was mellow enough that we had no qualms

about riding him. We brought out the saddle and began to bridle him. Here was where the honeymoon ended! Nicky hated the bridle as much as Shamrock hated the corral. By backing him into a corner of the shed, the athlete and I manhandled him into the bridle. Each and every time we ever rode him was a repeat of the same ordeal. You had to really want to ride to want to bridle Nicky.

Besides hating the bridle, Nicky had a few other vices. He was a spooky horse. Sometimes it was the mountain breeze and sometimes it was the flutter of an aspen leaf that spooked Nicky. When Nicky spooked, he ran like the wind until he was safe in his shed. The athlete had many a wild ride home when Nicky was spooked.

We owned Nicky through two long, cold, mountain winters. We lugged hay bales, broke ice on the water tank and chased chipmunks out of the molasses/grain barrel. We mucked out enough horse manure to fuel a fertilizer plant. We trimmed hooves, brushed burrs and paid a fortune in vet bills. Finally, the athlete and I agreed that horse ownership in the Rocky Mountains was more trouble than it was worth. We sold Nicky to a kid looking for a 4-H project for $125. He rode him home bareback. We smiled and closed the barn door after the horse had gone.

Chapter 8

MOUNTAIN DISASTERS

The actress and the athlete grew up to be quite capable young women. It was good that Ace and I gave them the edge in life by moving them to the mountain. They learned to overcome hardships early on. After five years on the mountain, they were prepared for anything life had to offer.

They learned to drive on Spindly Pines Drive. They were both excellent drivers. As they were always running late, they maneuvered the hairpin curves and switchbacks at breakneck speed. In addition to the rocks and the washboards, there was always the newly licensed to drive, wild-haired Mrs. Schnafner to look out for. Ten months out of the year there was the snow to contend with.

We learned early on that the weather forecast regarding the anticipated depth of snowfall "above 8,000 feet" was not a random dividing line. While I have not thoroughly researched the meteorological reason for this, I can tell you that the depth of the snowfall above 8,000 feet was at least a foot more per snowfall than it was below 8,000 feet. I know this because the 8,000 foot mark was about midway up Spindly Pines Drive. It was not easy to make it past that midway point on a snowy night.

Since Ace and I did not want to deprive our daughters of any city activities, all four of us spent a good deal of our lives driving up and down the mountain. Three out of the four of us had accidents doing it. Neither Ace nor our daughters were seriously injured in their automobile mishaps, but it was hard on cars.

We ended up with an entire fleet of Subaru four-wheel drive wagons. They were fairly stable, economical to drive and could plow their way up the mountain during a heavy snowfall. With Aspen loaded in the back for traction, we were also prepared for an avalanche.

As luck would have it, we never did have an avalanche. However, we did face any number of other natural and man-made disasters. The most frightening was a forest fire which raged out of control for a week. With the fire below us, we were packed and ready to leave the mountain at any time. The thick smoke was inescapable. It filled the air and burned our eyes and nostrils. Breathing was difficult and sleeping was frightening. We packed our most precious belongings and kept watch for the wind to shift. Slurry planes fought the blaze until it was out. The house and everything in it smelled like smoke for months.

Most of the man-made disasters were of our own doing. Many of them had to do with our lack of knowledge concerning the shifting of the terrain and the settling process of the logs. Besides the strange configuration of the cedar framework against the logs in various places, the fireplace turned out to be a major problem. The used brick, floor-to-ceiling fireplace wall was forever cracking. As the logs settled, the weight of the roof pushed against the upper tiers of bricks. Since the roof had the decided advantage, the bricks buckled under the pressure. The exterior bricks cracked along the mortar lines and leaned outward. The interior bricks pulled away from the wall and leaned forward. Looking up at them you definitely got the "Leaning Tower of Pisa" sensation. We wondered when they might topple over.

We were back in the mortar mixing business. Ace became a master at the mix and patch process. The problem was that while he filled the cracks and the mortar looked good, the bricks kept leaning outward. There was no telling when they might finally give in to gravity. We continued to mix and patch each spring after the house shifted during the spring thaw. If the bricks ever fell, we were not around to see them.

While the fireplace kept its distance, other things fell on a regular basis. I was into rustic in a big way. One kitchen wall was devoted to the rustic, mountain look. Instead of cabinets, I had open shelving. On the open shelving I set antique pottery jugs and fruit jar canisters. They were filled with coffee beans, flour, sugar, tea and any number of earthy, back-to-the-basics staples.

The biggest mess I ever saw happened while I was in Denver, thus the natural disaster behind it has remained a mystery. The result of the disaster was that (for some unknown reason) the jars of staples were knocked right off the open shelving, breaking the jars and spilling the contents in a heap on the kitchen floor. Years later, coffee beans were still working their way out of the oak plank flooring.

While that particular disaster was a mystery, a similar situation occurred several weeks later. I had just gotten replacements for the entire regiment of open shelving canisters. They were all filled and looking rustic when the neighbors began dynamite blasting for a basement. There was a repeat performance of the first disaster. By the time I cleaned up that mess, I had tired of the rustic look.

One of the problems with horizontal log walls is that no two logs are alike. Picture hanging is a real problem, especially with larger pictures. While the log at the appropriate picture hanging height may be eight inches in diameter, the one below it may be ten or twelve inches in diameter. Therefore, the picture is never exactly balanced. It may fall at the least provocation. Since dynamite blasts were fairly provocative, the pictures fell on a regular basis. They learned to roll with the fall. It was rather unsettling to return home to find them randomly scattered about the floor. You never could be sure if a neighbor had been blasting for a basement or if a robber had made a hasty retreat.

With picture hanging being such a precarious operation, my interior decorating style began to evolve toward the eclectic. Items not normally found in frame houses fit right into the scheme of things in our log house. My first treasure was Grandad Messer's thirty-gallon, black iron pot. It was the same pot he had used to wash my mother's baby clothes. After she married, my daddy dragged it out once a year at hog butchering time. It had rendered lard and made lye soap for our family my entire life. I remembered it well. The black pot became our kindling box.

When I dragged the pot from Daddy's barn, I discovered other primitive treasures. There were wooden cheese boxes, old horse collars, wagon single-tree hitches and antique tools galore. I hauled them all to Colorado as "rustic decor". Ace recognized a good thing when he saw it. Being the astute mathematician that he was, he quickly calculated that decor from the horse barn was a blamed sight cheaper than decor at the Ethan Allen Gallery. He jumped right on the bandwagon. Instead of his usual gifts of frilly nighties and lavish floral arrangements, it was back to the basics. One birthday his gift to me was three, old wooden crates, a plowshare screwed to a slab of barnwood (with a rusty chain for hanging) and a wooden beer case. Sometimes you can get too much of a good thing.

We never did get the panoramic view of the Rocky Mountains that we anticipated. Ace thinned out the lodgepole pines - a tree at a time- hoping to find the perfect western exposure of the snowcapped peaks. As he cut each tree, there was always another spindly, little trunk that blocked the view. We finally sacrificed the only decent tree we had, thinking it must surely be the culprit. While it did help, you still had to squint one eye, look on the south side of the bird feeder and angle back between the big Aspen trees to the north to get a peek at a snowcapped peak. Then it wasn't too clear whether it was a peak or the side of a mountain that you had sighted in on. Still, it was a nice enough view considering we looked at snowcapped peaks close-up at least nine months out of the year.

When the actress was fourteen, we moved into a sprawling, split-level, rental house in Denver. The previous tenants had left a tacky, wooden plaque on the wall. Since they were being evicted for non-payment of rent, they were in a hurry to leave. The actress hated the plaque and the house. I rescued the plaque. I gift wrapped it and gave it to her our first Christmas in the log house.

> "True friends are like diamonds,
>   precious but rare.
> False friends are like autumn leaves,
>   found everywhere."

There was a message there. The message I was sending was that she learned to love the Denver neighborhood and didn't want to leave it. I hoped she would learn to love the mountain. She never did.

She did find her niche in the high school drama club. She starred in its production her senior year, graduated and went away to college. The athlete and I were left at home to tend her cat. The cat died. We drove to Fort Collins in tears to break the news to the actress that her cat had died. The actress gave one of her funnier performances and managed to cheer us up. We drove home feeling better.

The biggest disaster of our life on the mountain wasn't easy to define. It was complicated and a long time coming. Like our fireplace, the relationship between Ace and me began to crack. Like death, the crack was permanent. It was hard to say when it started or when it was too late to patch it up. Somewhere along Spindly Pines Drive we lost track of each other.

We didn't fight or scream or yell that our marriage was slipping away. That would have been beneath us both. Southern dignity required a certain graciousness to any situation. We decided a divorce was the simplest way out. And so we parted, on Pearl Harbor Day in 1979, one month to the day after our twentieth wedding anniversary.

The athlete and I stayed in the log house. The actress was away at college. Ace rented an apartment in Denver. All of us were ready to leave the mountain. We listed the house for sale with the local realtor. The sign was posted at the top of the driveway. All our memories, our hopes and plans and dreams, our good times and our bad times - they were all there in that realtor's sign. I felt like a failure each time I saw it.

The athlete played sports and worked a part-time job. I met her coming and going on the mountain. I waited up nights to be sure she got home safely. One night I fell asleep on the couch. The volunteer mountain firemen woke me, knocking on the door. The athlete had driven off the side of the road several hours earlier and was still unconscious. I rode to the Denver hospital with her in the ambulance. Ace met us there. Together we waited throughout the night. By morning the athlete was awake and none the worse for her mishap. It was as close as we came to being a family again.

Ace and I taught our daughters to respect the rights of others. They respected our right to find our own way separate and apart from each other. In later years, they said it was the worst time of their lives. At the time, they coped or pretended to. In the emotional turmoil the athlete bought a sports car. In a moment of weakness we let her.

The sports car was a white, MG Midget convertible. It was the athlete's pride and joy. It was good that she loved it so much, since the care and feeding of the sports car took her entire paycheck. During the fall the athlete was in her glory zipping around the mountains with the top down, loading her little car with tennis rackets and football players. Once the snow started falling, the little Midget had a tough time. It was definitely not a winter car. The athlete and I struggled to keep the Midget rolling. It was a Shamrock and Nicky situation all over again - one of the athlete's more expensive lessons. She eventually sold the sports car for a loss and continued to make payments on the loan long after the Midget rolled away.

Sometime during the Midget education, we recaptured our sense of humor. Proverbs were created by the score. Ace and I were swinging singles who had long ago forgotten how to swing. We tried hard to learn to swing again.

The subject of divorce is usually spoken of in terms of weepy or tacky. Given the choice, I will usually opt for tacky. It is always the safer ground. In retrospect, any number of proverbs come to mind. The one that most appropriately fits always seems to be the old adage, "Hindsight is 20/20."

The lessons Ace and I learned regarding marriage and divorce could fill many a counselor's manual. Somehow we got through the process and remained friends. In later years we saw our daughters marry, sitting side by side in church. As first the actress and later the athlete said their vows, I looked at their father beside me and remembered a log cabin on Spindly Pines Drive.

PART 11

CHAPTER 9

THE "OTHER" HOUSE

While our Spindly Pines neighbors didn't spend a lot of time socializing amongst themselves, they were a nosey lot. The "For Sale" sign was no sooner posted in our yard than Lena Olafson stopped to ask why. I saw no reason to keep secrets. I told her about the pending divorce. She exclaimed about the "amazing coincidence" with the "other" log house. I wasn't aware of any coincidence since the two identical houses were built within two miles of each other five years before. Lena couldn't wait to tell me that the blonde, Nordic beauty had left the engineer. Their house was also listed for sale by the local realtor. The sign had just been posted. As they say, truth is stranger than fiction.

Needless to say, any and all prospective buyers of log homes on our mountain were shown both our houses. Ace and I had the disadvantage in that the engineer's home was priced several thousand dollars less than ours was. Since he had erected his own log shell, he didn't need to recapture as large an investment.

I disliked him all over again. All the building time he cost Ace and me came flooding back in resentment. I remembered the high ceilings of his loft bedrooms every time I bumped my head in ours. Every frustration could somehow manifest itself in another reason to dislike the #*!* engineer.

Log home buyers are a peculiar lot. They came in pairs with two opposing tastes. Either the wife loved the rustic look and the husband had reservations or the husband was sold and the wife dragged her feet. The decision to buy a log home is always based on emotion. There is something about being surrounded by log walls that touches a chord in the hearts of home buyers. Each chord played a different tune. It was enough to make a grown man cry. When I finally ran into the engineer on the mountain, he looked like he had run the gamut with log home shoppers. He was a shadow of his former self. I hadn't seen him close up in several years. I was shocked at his appearance. He had lost a great deal of weight, had dark circles under his eyes and looked like he could use a decent meal. I mentally deleted the #*!* from the "#*!* engineer" in my thought pattern. The man looked like he needed all the help he could get.

As looker after looker trailed through our log homes, the engineer and I began to compare notes.

"What did they say about your house?"

"Do you think they will make an offer?"

"What did the realtor say?"

"Are you going to reduce your price?"

"Do you want to go to dinner?"

One thing led to another. I celebrated my birthday with a cake full of candles, baked by the engineer in the "other" house. His gift of a pair of cross country skis was the beginning of a relationship.

The engineer was different than anyone I had ever known. Most of the differences arose from his Minnesota upbringing. He loved Minnesota so much that I wondered why he was living on a Colorado mountain. His spirit seemed rekindled as he told me of the clear, northern lakes full of fish and the melody of loon music.

The engineer talked of his German heritage, oom-pa-pa polka bands and dark, German beer. He loved a rollicking good time and still believed in Friday night dates. I hadn't been on a Friday night date since Ace and I were in college. His northern Minnesota lifestyle sounded like fun. My lifestyle needed some fun.

Both Ace and my mother began reciting proverbs to me.

"You're getting out of the frying pan and into the fire." (My mother)

"Look before you leap, Babe." (Ace)

"You can't go home again."
(Larren quoting Thomas Wolfe)

"Don't bite off more than you can chew."
(My mother)

"Let the good times roll!" (Larren)

As usual, I leaped before I looked. Certainly I bit off more than I could chew. In later years, I looked back and asked why. I never did come up with the answer. The nearest I ever came to the truth was that I had been married since I was nineteen years old. By the time I was forty, I didn't know how not to be married. The engineer was simply the other half of the equation.

Like a soap opera, the saga continued. The log houses didn't sell. We didn't receive a single offer on either one of them. Ace returned to Spindly Pines and bought my share of our log home. The athlete and I moved to Evergreen. We rented a tiny, furnished log cabin on the banks of Bear Creek. I moved my furniture to the engineer's house just down the mountain.

It was late fall with winter coming soon. The athlete and I were happy that we didn't have to drive the icy mountain to get home. Her little Midget had a tough time getting up Spindly Pines Drive. It should have been a time to reflect, to be close, to just be still and enjoy the season. We might have made it if it hadn't been

98

Thanksgiving and then Christmas. The holidays drew us back to the mountain - her to decorate a tree for Ace and me to the substitute "other" home I had found. My furniture was a powerful draw.

In January, the engineer and I were married. The athlete was my attendant. Our wedding was in a log church beside a stream in the Rocky Mountains. All our children, the engineer's German mother and various friends witnessed the occasion. The athlete's first serious boyfriend took the wedding pictures. He was a camera buff. Looking at the pictures later, I realized his was the only sincere smile in all the pictures. It was one of his first photographic assignments, so he had a reason to smile.

Coming home to the "other" house after the wedding was an humbling experience. As if coming to the wrong log house wasn't bad enough, I slipped on the icy driveway and fell flat on my behind in all my wedding finery. I figured there was an omen there somewhere.

Ours was not exactly a match made in heaven. The engineer was a Yankee, German Catholic. I was a Southern, Scotch/Irish Protestant. I took pride in my Southern cooking. He liked Minnesota hot dishes. I called them casseroles and served steak and potatoes. (He did enjoy my chicken-fried steak until he realized it was steak instead of chicken.) My holiday dinners included cornbread dressing and giblet gravy. His Yankee dressing was a soggy mixture of white bread, ground beef and carrots. It closely resembled a hot dish.

He was an avid skier and challenged the elements. I sat by the fire and read a book. I loved the written word and often used words as my weapons. His reading habits were restricted to engineering texts. He scoffed at those who "talked a good game". I lived in Levis, he liked preppie clothes. He loved wool, I had an affinity for cotton. To him, Southerners were phony. To me, Yankees were cold and lacking social graces. And so it went.

It was the Civil War all over again and we weren't just whistling "Dixie". I was determined that the South would rise again. Any sensible woman would have packed up and gone home and to hell with Thomas Wolfe and his proverbs. However, pride is a dangerous thing. I was not about to admit to being wrong, especially to Ace and my mother. I figured I had made my bed and I would lie in it. By that time, I had invested the money Ace had given me in the "other" house. Even after my investment, it continued to be the "other" house.

Despite the spacious loft bedrooms, I was never comfortable in the house. It was similar to mine, but not mine. I wondered how I could ever have compared my house to this one and found mine lacking. I pined for my narrow, dark living room with the funny cedar curves falling all over the place. The leaning, brick fireplace was truly a work of art. The horse corral in the back was a beautiful clearing. The perfect, miniature view of the Rockies at the angle between the bird feeder and the aspen trees was more beautiful than the most panoramic horizon. The engineer's chinking was too neat and narrow. The massive logs needed massive chinking for balance. And so it went.

The athlete and I remained close, as close as we could be while living in different houses. For a time she slept in the spacious loft bedroom she could stand up in. I'm sure she felt no more at home there than I did and missed her cozy, lemon yellow carpet. She said that Ace needed her more than I did. I had to agree. I still felt an intense loyalty to him myself. I looked after the athlete even though she lived in her father's house. Sometimes the "looking after" included Ace as well, albeit unknown to both him and the engineer. It was a tangled web.

Laundry was my most critical test. Since the athlete was busy with school, sports, a job and taking care of her father's house, I usually attended to her laundry. On occasion, Ace's clothes ended up in the laundry basket. I worried that his jockey shorts would find their way into the stack of the engineer's boxers or vice versa. Shirts were even trickier. They wore the same size, matching oxford-cloth, button-down collars. Sometimes it was a case of Eeny, Meeny, Miney, Moe.

A key player in the game at my "other" house was the engineer's sixteen-year old son. He lived with us most of the time. He was a likeable kid going through the normal sixteen-year old problems. Since I was the mother of daughters, I hadn't the vaguest notion how to handle a sixteen-year old boy. It didn't come easy, but then nothing ever did. I was having enough trouble juggling two daughters, a job, a St. Bernard, the Yankee engineer and Ace's laundry.

The engineer was a good, decent man. It was a shame we came from opposite poles. Home and family were the most important things in the world to him. It was probably the reason he resorted to marrying a Southern wife. He was trying hard to make a home for his son. He missed his daughter who lived with her mother. He encouraged her to join us. Except for visits, she never did.

The engineer and I realized early on that our marriage would never survive if we stayed in the log house. It finally sold and we moved to Denver. It was about the same time that Ace's log house sold. He also moved to Denver. The actress was in college at Fort Collins. The athlete went to fashion merchandising school in Denver and visited both of us often.

Looking back on the months I lived in the "other" log house, it is hard to remember. It was a beautiful, custom home. The engineer was a perfectionist with an eye for detail. His cabinetry was handmade, blending perfectly with the mellow, honey pine logs. His sense of proportion was everywhere - from the spacious, loft bedrooms to the symmetrical, narrow lines of concrete chinking. His deck overlooked the lights of Denver. His carpeting was a bright, homey plaid. His fireplace stood straight and tall.

The engineer tried hard to make his log house my home. My dark pine furniture was beautiful in the well-proportioned rooms. I was given free rein to decorate. Beautiful that it was, it never felt like home. Maybe because my home was two miles up the hill and it was hard to have two homes. Finally, we left Spindly Pines - the engineer and I. The matching log houses that brought us together became just an interesting story to tell.

I didn't go back to the mountain for several years. When I went, I held a baby granddaughter on my lap. I said, "Susie, there's the house that your Grandpa Ace and I built." The dark, russet brown logs were still dark and the leaning, brick fireplace was still standing. The spindly little pines hadn't grown a lot. The clearing of the horse corral was still clear. It still felt like coming home. I didn't drive past the "other" house.

CHAPTER 10

MOVING ON

The ten years I spent with the engineer were an "Adventure in Moving" from start to finish. I became so adept at moving, I could have gone to work for U-Haul. Our first move to a Denver condominium was just the start of something big. After that we didn't let too much grass grow under our feet. By the time we got to Denver, the engineer's son had gone to live with his mother. The actress and the athlete were out on their own. The engineer began to talk about Minnesota again. He interviewed for a job in Minnesota. Within months we were packing to move to Minnesota.

Leaving Colorado was hard. The engineer and I traveled in separate cars when we moved. He went ahead while I took care of packing and moving. After he had gone, I almost didn't go. At the last minute I loaded up the car, packed the athlete's cat and started my trek to the north country. The cat did not travel well nor silently. It was a toss-up as to who cried the most on our cross-country trek, the cat or me.

We bought a house in Minnesota, a big split-level affair in a small, farming community. It was just another house that never got to be a home. Within months, the Denver firm where the engineer had worked called with an offer from their Canadian office. It was an offer too good to refuse. The athlete's cat and I were off to Calgary, Alberta.

Canada was a new experience. I was especially careful not to use the term "you all" north of the border. We lived in a rented house and spent week-ends trekking to the Canadian Rockies. We stayed in quaint log cabins called Cedar Chalets and skied on glaciers. The battles of Vicksburg and Gettysburg continued to rage on.

Trips to Denver were fairly frequent, usually for major events. First the actress, then the athlete married. First the actress, then the athlete had babies. The little hostages were named Steve and Susie.

The engineer was assigned between Denver and Calgary for two years. From there we moved to the Gila Wilderness Area in New Mexico. We lived in a picturesque adobe house at the edge of the Gila. The adobe was an architect's dream home, complete with stained-glass kitchen windows and a royal blue, sunken tile bathtub in an atrium-style bathroom. It was earthy, original and comfortable. It was the first time I felt at home since I shared the log house with Ace and my daughters.

I loved New Mexico with its chile farms and southwest flavor. The Spanish culture and cuisine was a rare treat after the cool reserve of the north country. Pinon pine trees dotted the desert landscape around the adobe. The Gila Wilderness Area was a short hike away. Within miles, massive Ponderosa pines and Douglas fir were thick and tall. Quail and coyotes roamed the wilderness. Nights were crisp and cool. The pungent fragrance of pinon smoke filled the air.

Midway through the New Mexico assignment, I had a routine Pap smear. Within a week, I had surgery for cervical cancer. The day I was released from the hospital, my grandson (two-year old Steve) was admitted to a Denver hospital. He was in an automobile accident and had a head injury. I remembered all the bad times when the actress had come through with a cheerful performance. I hoped she could manage one more as she hovered at his bedside. Both Steve and I recuperated. I stitched proverbs in needlepoint for the actress and the athlete. By the time I finished the proverbs, the athlete gave birth to Mike. I welcomed the brown-eyed imp into the world in a Denver hospital delivery room. Soon after Mike's birth, the engineer received another assignment to Calgary.

During the Calgary assignment we bought a house. Our neighborhood adjoined a wilderness park and was quite affluent. The house had been neglected and needed updating. Since both the engineer and I had built log houses, we felt up to the task. The biggest problem was that the engineer and I had never built a house together. It soon became apparent that our crew did not work well together.

The engineer was working at the most northern Canadian outpost. He came home week-ends to

107

supervise the remodeling project. I was to accomplish the grunt work during the week while he was gone. Week-ends were not a lot of fun.

The engineer prefaced his instructions with, "Now, Larren, you have to, etc." I wondered if he copied my mother's proverb salutation, hoping for the same effect. For an intelligent man, in the ten years we were together it was surprising that he never learned that Larren never did anything because she had to. I was a rebel with a cause - the cause being to retain my rebel independence. Ace learned that early on. The more closely I worked with the engineer, the fonder my memories became of Ace as a building contractor. Chipboard and pink fiberglass insulation haunted my dreams. They were always overwhelmed by sheetrock dust and three layers of old wallpaper glue. This was a classy neighborhood where we lived. We were striving for the same classy look. Everything was done in shades of neutral; off-white walls, beige kitchen tile, plushy wheat carpet, winter-white drapes, almond kitchen appliances. It was a nondescript house totally lacking in color and personality. The engineer was striving for a perfectly finished, white elephant. He demanded skilled craftsmanship from his Okie day laborer. Many was the time I cried alligator tears while I re-did jobs that didn't meet his standards of excellence.

The particular job that comes to mind regarding multiple re-dos was the window wall across the front of the living room. While we never planned to live in that particular white room, we did want it to show well when realtors entered the house. We had learned our lessons regarding realtors at Spindly Pines. The engineer thought the long, narrow windows should be surrounded by white, gloss-enameled frames, thus making the windows appear larger by not breaking up the monochromatic color scheme. I was left with the job of stripping the window frames and applying three coats of white, gloss enamel. I worked diligently on the window frames, carefully brushing on the enamel exactly as the engineer had instructed. When the white enamel dried, there was a faint design of brush strokes. I anxiously awaited the week-end inspection.

Just as I anticipated, the engineer wasn't overly impressed with the brush stroke pattern.

"Now, Larren, you have to re-do these windows."

I cried and stripped three layers of enamel. I repeated the entire series of applications (complete with brush stroke designs). The next two weeks we repeated the entire process. After the third week's inspection failure, I threw my paintbrush in exasperation at the *#!* engineer.

"If you want the *#!* window frames done differently, you can do it your *#!* self!"

I stormed out of the house.

The engineer took great pains in stripping and applying the white enamel. When he finished the third coat, his brush strokes were even more visible than mine had been. Being a logical man, the engineer consulted the expert at the paint store where he had purchased the enamel. He was told by the expert, "That's the nature of the beast. If you can't handle a few brush strokes, you better get a different type of enamel."

Score one for the rebel.

We lived with the refurbishing mess in the Calgary house even longer than we lived with the building mess on the mountain. I got used to the scaffolding and ladders. I became so conditioned to the sheet rock dust that I had a difficult time breathing regular air. I still get a high from the smell of old wallpaper paste. After more than a year, I hung the last of the fancy, winter-white drapes. The realtor nailed his sign in the yard the following day. I wondered what sort of colorless family would want to live in a house decorated in eight shades of neutral. A pilot bought the house. Needless to say, he had no wife or children. He was accustomed to a white cockpit in a neutral, Canadian sky with the snow-capped Rockies below. To each his own, I always say.

CHAPTER 11

COPING

Before I was a cancer survivor, I took a lot of things for granted. A healthy body was one of those things. After the surgery, I had a different sort of perspective. While I counted my blessings, I began to feel invincible. I had met the enemy head-on and he was mine. I felt ready to take on anything. That feeling came to an abrupt halt after another doctor's cancer diagnosis. That cancer wasn't mine. It belonged to my dad, the jovial Irishman to whom I credited my sense of humor.

Without a doubt, all daughters feel their relationship with their father is something rare and special. I knew mine was. My dad was both my idol and my nemesis. He was a red-faced, Scotch/Irish tease cackling with laughter when he properly put me in my place. I was a smaller, feminine version of him. From the time I was a toddler, I heard his favorite saying, "You're getting too big for your britches, Knothead. I'm going to have to take you down a notch or two." That was usually followed by, "If I give you an inch, you take a mile." He was always proudest of me when I was "too big for my britches". He never did succeed in taking me down a notch or two. I doubt that he ever really tried.

My dad was the yardstick by which I measured all men. They always came up lacking. From the time I could remember, he was a key player in my favorite memories. My mother and I tagged after him wherever he went - whether he was hunting squirrels or milking the cows. My most outstanding early memory concerned a walk in the cow pasture that turned into a skunk hunt. Mother and I had gone with Daddy to drive the cows in for milking time. He always carried a twenty-two rifle in case he saw a cotton-tailed rabbit along the way. Many was the time we came home with a young rabbit or squirrel to fry for supper. That particular night Daddy shot at a squirrel. The shot aroused a rather large family of skunks. There were skunks of all shapes and sizes scurrying all over the pasture, at least seven or eight of the stinking varmints. I don't recall the smell as much as I recall Mother's panic. It was one of our more exciting hunts.

My dad was called "Scotch" by his eleven brothers and sisters. He didn't believe in wasting good money on frivolous things. During my teen-age years, most of my waking thoughts were of frivolous things. Mother didn't have a lot of frivolous things during her teen-age years, so she indulged most of my whims. We spent many hours shopping and buying pretty clothes. I always managed to set my heart on something at the high end of the budget. She always bought whatever I had my heart set on, prefacing the purchase with, "Now, Larren, don't tell your daddy what we paid for this." Of course I couldn't wait to tell Daddy exactly what we paid for it.

After all, what pleasure could I possibly get from the thing if I couldn't aggravate Daddy regarding its price?

My boyfriends were a challenge all of their own where my dad was concerned. When my mother was fourteen, Daddy chased down one of her best boyfriends and stuck his head in a horse tank. He still cackled with laughter as he told the story of Mother's half-drowned boyfriend in his Sunday-go-to-meetin' clothes. I was never sure that he might not do the same thing with my dates. I tried to hustle them in and out quickly, however I was between a rock and a hard place.

In the fifties, girls played at being hard to get. Part of the scenario was keeping your date waiting when he came to pick you up, so as not to appear overly anxious. They were forced to cool their heels in the family living room making small talk with your parents until you felt the proper length of time had lapsed. Then you made a grand appearance - acting as if you hadn't been ready to go and cooling your heels for the last hour. It was the way the game was played.

I felt the proper waiting time was fifteen minutes. Any less would have given the boy an unfair advantage. Any more would have tried his patience. Those had to be the longest fifteen minutes any teen-age boy ever spent, being interrogated by my dad. The city boys I chose were at a decided disadvantage. They knew absolutely nothing about the subjects they needed to.

Daddy started with livestock. His herd of red and white Shorthorn cows was his pride and joy. (The farm boys fared fairly well at this point.) After livestock, he progressed to the daily newscasts. We were one of the more well informed farm families. My dad listened to or watched a full two hours of local and national news each and every day of his life. Whether the 6:00 p.m. lead stories were on war, politics or crime, my date was expected to be up to the minute with his coverage. This was where you could separate the men from the boys. Most of them flunked that particular test. If by chance they did pass, Daddy rose to the challenge. From there he progressed to their feelings regarding crop rotation, pork commodities and grain futures. Between my tests regarding the family hog truck and his tests concerning world events, it's a wonder I ever found a suitable husband.

My dad's cancer diagnosis came shortly after the engineer and I purchased a resort in northern Minnesota. It wasn't just a little cancer that the doctor could cut out and you could feel invincible about. It was massive and invasive. It was too late to do much but accept it and learn to live with it. Daddy went home to work his farm and tend to his Shorthorn cows. The doctors gave him three or four months to do it.

The engineer and I embarked on our new resorting career with high hopes. If we had trying times before the resort, as they say, "You ain't seen nuthin' yet." I gathered enough material to fill a book. As if a business I knew nothing about, thirteen cabins that could best be described as a handyman's nightmare and a North vs. South marriage wasn't enough, now I had a cancer to deal with. I didn't deal with it well.

114

Death, up close and personal, was a new experience for me. While several of my older relatives had passed on, I had remained far enough removed from it that I had not been much affected. I didn't know how to deal with it or accept it. I didn't like that either. At first I cried buckets of tears. Then I lashed out in anger at anyone or anything who happened to get in my way - the cat, the engineer, the beer cooler, the doctors, whatever. They all bore the brunt of my frustration. In the midst of all the turmoil, my beloved Grandad (my mother's daddy) took the flu and died. Within months, Ace's mother (who had been like my own mother for twenty years) also died. Death was all around me. I never knew there was so much death in the world.

The engineer dealt with the weeping, miserable mess he called his wife the same way he always did. "Now, Larren, you have to learn to cope with this." That was usually followed by his standard lecture regarding phony Southerners and their inability to do anything right - be it cope, paint, run a resort, etc. We had many a coping battle before he sent me home to visit my parents in Oklahoma.

By that time, my dad had healed from the surgery that found the beast in his belly. He was tending his cows and riding his tractor. I was still lashing out at all of life's unfairness. Calmly and matter of factly, that Irishman looked me square in the eye. He said, "Nobody ever said life would be fair, Knothead." And so I learned to cope.

It's a good thing we all learned to cope, because Daddy lived another full year longer than the doctor said he would. It would have been pretty tiresome if we'd all sat around feeling sorry for ourselves. As it was, I had several long visits with my dad. We never discussed the cancer or the coping. Instead, we busied ourselves with finding the biggest, crispest Red Delicious apples in the basket at the grocery store or watched for quail to shoot along his tree row.

Daddy relied on his gray Ford tractor to carry him where he normally walked. He took care of his Shorthorn cows and moved hay bales - all with the help of his tractor. He lived quietly and simply as he had always lived, taking for granted the hand that life had dealt him. He didn't complain or feel sorry for himself or give us any final, last wish instructions. He faced death just as he embraced life, with his Irish sense of humor and Southern style. After spending his lifetime teaching me how to live, he spent his last year showing me how to die - with dignity and grace.

Finally, Daddy died - on Pearl Harbor Day in 1988 - a year and four months after the doctor's diagnosis. I remembered another Pearl Harbor Day almost twenty years before when Ace and I sat in a Colorado divorce court. It was the same kind of feeling that I had.

I sat in the Southern Baptist Church and listened to the pastor eulogize the cackling, red-faced Irishman. Instead of the engineer, it was Ace who sat beside me. Between us sat a cute, blue-eyed blonde - our granddaughter, Susie. Ace drew smiley faces on the funeral program. Susie giggled and I scowled at them both. In the pew behind us, the actress and the athlete were taken back twenty years to other smiley faces drawn by their father and other scowls by their mother. We all coped and went home to our other lives.

CHAPTER 12

FAMILY RESORTS

Resort vacations evoke fond memories in native Minnesotans who are exposed to them early on in life. My exposure to a Minnesota resort vacation did not happen early on in my life. It happened when I was forty years old and had a preconceived notion of what entailed a proper resort. To say that my expectations were not met would have been a gross understatement.

During our time together, the engineer and I traveled extensively. The only thing we consistently agreed upon was the style of lodging we selected. We stayed in rustic, mountain retreats from Mexico to British Columbia. They were typical of a Colorado ski lodge, rustic but tasteful. We loved the homey look and warm feeling of real wood, either in log walls or wood paneling. We looked for cabins and lodges with a fireplace or wood stove. Decorating was mellow, subdued and woodsy. Whenever our chosen retreat was outfitted with handmade, log furniture, it received our five-star rating. We had several favorites in our cross-country skiing jaunts. There was no confusion about our idea of the perfect cabin in the woods.

Since we were in complete agreement on this particular subject, whenever the engineer talked of the northern Minnesota resorts that he loved, it was easy for me to picture them in my mind. His brown eyes grew misty when he talked of the haunting echo of loons calling through the foggy dawn or the evening twilight, locating their mates across the lake. I was as touched as he was by the idea of this bit of heaven on earth.

The resort lodge would take the form of a larger version of our log house - with a few mounted deer and moose on the massive, log walls. The resort cabins would be a smaller version of our house, rustic and tasteful. They would be decorated in earthtones with a touch of color here and there to brighten things up. Bedspreads and curtains would be plaid in shades of the autumn woods. Blankets would be Hudson Bay wool with bold stripes in red and black. There would be a woodstove or cobblestone fireplace and a braided rag rug on the polished wood floor.

The resort guests were easy to picture. They were in the pages of Eddie Bauer and L.L. Bean catalogs. They wore red-plaid flannel or chamois shirts with khaki walking shorts or denim jeans. They had a woodsman's cap set at a jaunty angle above a casual, outdoor hairstyle. They carried a fly rod or a canoe as they portaged through the spruce woods. They were comfortable in their Gortex hiking boots, happy to escape civilization and its confines.

My first look at a Minnesota resort took place the summer after I married the engineer. While he usually camped in the rugged Boundary Waters Canoe Area, he planned the perfect resort vacation for his new bride. He selected a "family" resort geared to planned family activities. The reason for this choice was our two youngest daughters who were joining us on the trip to Minnesota. The athlete wasn't overly excited about the trip. She had recently graduated from high school and had other things on her mind. I bribed her to come along. Her photographer/boyfriend was working at a resort near Brainerd, Minnesota. I said I would take her to visit him.

When the engineer's German mother heard we were vacationing in northern Minnesota, she decided to join us. The engineer didn't have the heart to refuse. Ours was a rather unique, extended-family resort vacation.

The resort was indeed geared to planned family activities. It had some sort of scheduled activity going on every hour of the day. There were pot luck picnics, bonfires, card parties, nature hikes, skits, bingo and scheduled water skiing. It was not the Northwoods retreat I had pictured. We had all the comforts of home and about as much privacy as the local Y.M.C.A.

The one thing that we did not have at the resort during the entire week was a fish fry. Since I had heard numerous tales of the legendary Minnesota walleye, I was dying to taste one of the things. The closest we got to a walleye was the mount on the wall at a local restaurant. The engineer attempted to buy a walleye from the resort owner. She gave him a rather scathing look - as if I probably wasn't his wife and he needed

121

some fishing evidence to take home to the one who waited there.

I have to give the engineer credit. He worked at catching fish. He regressed from being a sophisticated fly fisherman with a stylish technique to scouting for spawning beds with a bobber and worms. The only fish we were able to capture happened to be mine. The taking of the fish was a story in itself.

I hooked a three-pound northern pike on my bobber and worm. As I maneuvered the fish to the boat, it broke the line and escaped. The engineer paddled around the lily pads searching for the bobber. It surfaced a good half hour later. That's when the chase began. The fish-hungry engineer rowed the boat into the thick lily pads in pursuit of the elusive fish. The bobber of the broken line tangled in the carpet of lily pads. Our remaining fishing lines (which had been forgotten when the chase began) also tangled in the thick lily pads. I made a valiant leap for the bobber with the fish attached, very nearly upsetting the boat in the process. The engineer steadied the boat with one oar while I clubbed the fish with the other oar. We hauled the northern pike on board. Now until this point, I had never had any dealings with a northern pike. I was unaware that they are equipped with sharp teeth. I proudly hefted my pike to the stringer by his mouth and gills. The dazed pike clamped down on my fingers with its sharp teeth. Blood sprayed the boat. It was a rather colorful snapshot of my first northern pike.

Ours was not the most successful family resort vacation. The engineer wanted to show me his beloved

Minnesota northwoods. We wanted our daughters to be close. We often left them alone, hoping for the bonding to happen. We never did get anywhere near Brainerd and the athlete's boyfriend. The only success the entire week happened at the Wednesday night bingo game when the engineer's mother won the $3 pot. We were all relieved when the week was finally over. It was a long drive back to Colorado.

We didn't go near a Minnesota family resort for years. The engineer still talked of loons and walleye. We moved from state to state, country to country. We continued to seek lodging in rustic, off-the-beaten-path resorts and ski lodges. Our marriage was not exactly thriving. We looked for ways to make it better. The engineer felt his beloved Minnesota northwoods would make anything better. Each September the glories of the autumn woods haunted him. He sometimes went to Minnesota alone.

It was on a fall fishing vacation that he ventured near family resorts again. He called me in Colorado to tell me of his wanderings. One rainy day he stopped at a realtor's office. The realtor happened to have the listing for a 13-cabin resort on a good walleye lake. The price had just been reduced. He wanted to know how I felt about buying a resort. How I felt was, "No way in HELL!" I delivered the line with the same finality that Rhett Butler told Scarlett O'Hara, "Quite frankly, my dear, I don't give a damn." In retrospect, that would have been my reply. However, at the time he caught me unprepared.

Since the engineer had never gone so far as to consult a realtor in the past, I assumed he must be serious. I flew to Minnesota to see what he was up to. We drove to see his family resort of choice. If I was disappointed in our first resort vacation, the best was yet to come. This family resort had about as much in common with a rustic, northwoods retreat as home brew does to champagne. It was a hybrid cross between a miniature golf course and Disneyland. Cute little, painted deer cutouts decorated each and every building. Whirligigs abounded. Exterior colors were in every hue of the rainbow. Interior cabin decoration was a series of plastic flowers stapled to birch logs. They sat on tables, they hung on walls. Birch logs were everywhere except in a fireplace or woodstove. The cabins didn't have fireplaces or woodstoves. The "NO WAY IN HELL!" line echoed across the lake.

As the last hhheeellllll echo drifted across the lake, a curious loon popped out of the water to look my way. Now in the past I had no more dealings with loons than I had with pike. The only reference to loons I had ever heard was when some Okie hillbilly said, "Old so and so is crazy as a loon." Now here was this loon looking at me like I was the crazy one. Then as if that wasn't bad enough, that crazy loon began to laugh at me - a high-pitched, eerie sounding laugh. I had never heard such a sound. I could understand why these loons were called crazy. It was the wildest sound I had ever heard. It reminded me of the coyotes howling at night in Oklahoma. I hustled the engineer out of that family resort and away from that laughing loon as quickly as I could.

The engineer explained about the different loon calls. Instead of crazy laughing, he called them yodels, hoots and tremolos. I talked about loons at length, so as to avoid talking about the family resort idea. We packed our bags and started driving back to Colorado where lodges and cabins were tasteful and rustic and the wildlife didn't laugh at you.

To this day I cannot explain my change in attitude on that drive home. The more I thought of having our own business, the more I liked the idea. I loved to sew and decorate. If there ever was a place that needed a decorator's touch, it was this particular family resort. I could wear my beloved Levis every day of the week and design my own sweatshirt with my name on it to match. I would paint those multi-colored cabins a dark, russet brown and burn the birch logs with plastic flowers. I would show that loon he couldn't laugh at an Okie and get away with it. My mother always said, "He who laughs last, laughs best." I would have the last laugh on that loon after all.

And so I became a family resort owner in the Minnesota northwoods. The engineer and I quit our jobs and embarked on our new business. During the month after we completed the resort purchase, the athlete scheduled a doctor's appointment for Mike. The brown-eyed imp was past two years old by then. He did not seem to be developing language and other skills at the

125

rate of his sister who was a mere fifteen months older than him. I hoped that little boys just developed at a different pace than little girls. I loved him dearly. The doctor's diagnosis was the dreaded word "autism". Just how severe the degree of autism, only time would tell. If leaving Colorado the first time was hard, leaving the athlete with the newly diagnosed autistic toddler and his not much older sister was virtually impossible. It was definitely a case of having to lie in the bed I had made.

I got through the ordeal by telling myself that one day Mike would develop vocal skills and that he would love to visit Grandma's resort in the Northwoods. I pictured Susie, Mike and me tearing around the lake in a speed boat, catching fish and swimming in the clear, northern waters. As it turned out, that's exactly the way it happens each summer. Mike is an intelligent, witty and quite vocal eleven-year old now. He is my kindred spirit. Susie is his mentor, his nemesis and his teacher as well as his sister. Together in the resort speed boat, we are a formidable team.

Before leaving Colorado I bought any item of decorating that was rustic, woodsy and inexpensive. I located a mill end fabric outlet that sold high quality cottons for $1 a pound. I bought an entire trainload of beige fabric that can only be described as cotton sacking material. I imagine some Southern cotton plantation was without picking sacks that year because of my purchase. All the cabin windows sported floral, fiberglass draperies. They would be the first item to go. In their place, the windows would be covered with tab top curtains of the cotton sack fabric hung on heavy, wooden dowel rods.

I bought mill ends of upholstery materials in autumn shades of russet, gold, green and brown. Many were plaid. They all blended and could be used in any of the cabins, interchangeably. I found a blanket factory outlet which specialized in a less expensive copy of Canadian Hudson Bay blankets. I splurged on blankets for each cabin. I bought wall decorations of natural materials, grapevine wreaths and wicker. I ordered several sets of inexpensive, wildlife prints and matted them in barnwood frames. When we left Colorado, half the moving van was filled with interior decorating supplies.

We bought the resort when autumn leaves served as a glorious camouflage. When we returned in November, the bleak awakening can best be described as a repeat of the Spindly Pines lot after the snow melt. I was heartsick when I saw it. It was far worse than I remembered. The engineer and I had no choice but to make the best of what we had. I began to upholster couches and sew curtains. He began to repair plumbing and build a game room. Proverbs flew fast and furiously. It was a long, cold winter.

Gradually, the cabin interiors took on the look I was striving for. Every scrap of fabric and every item of decoration blended to create the rustic Northwoods image I had pictured. The engineer's game room was the best constructed building on the entire resort. It was rustic and charming. When we opened for business in May, our returning guests were amazed at the transformation.

My education regarding life in the north country didn't come easy. Some things were fairly simple. Some were uphill all the way. The Norwegian and Finnish ethnic cultures of our neighbors were foreign to me. Since the engineer was a native Minnesotan and German, I assumed I was coming to a land of dark beer and polka music. When I encountered lefse and lutefisk, I was totally unprepared. To make matters worse, I was introduced to these strange foods at a Lutheran Church dinner. With the entire assembly watching my reaction, the lutefisk actually stuck in my throat. At least I was prepared with a number of Ole and Lena jokes after living near the Olafsons in Spindly Pines for a number of years. My Minnesota Norwegian neighbors had no way of knowing the jokes happened in Colorado.

Our family resort operated in much the same way as the other family resort I had experienced. This time I was the camp counselor, bingo caller, bartender, pot luck hostess, nature hike guide, fishing contest weigh-in person, etc. Actually, it was a case of every man for himself at the weekly fishing contest weigh-in. The job rotated between the engineer, the hired dock boy and me - depending on who had managed to find the best hiding place. The engineer or I usually weighed fish since the dock boy knew all the best hiding places. It was a long, hot summer.

After one season of resorting, the engineer decided it wasn't all it was cracked up to be. He called a realtor and went to engineer on Johnson Island. I stayed in Minnesota, first to sell the resort I had come to love and then to work a job promoting tourism to the north country. I rented a house in the country near Big Mantrap Lake. It was a peaceful existence with the engineer away. I began to look at other resorts.

The engineer didn't settle into life on Johnson Island easily. He missed Minnesota and he missed home. He said he missed his wife as well, although for the life of me I couldn't imagine why. I certainly hadn't given him any reason to. Maybe he had become a Civil War buff during our years together. For whatever reason, he came home during the fall of our tenth year together. The Minnesota northwoods were beautiful that time of the year. We looked at resorts together. We tried hard to reach a ceasefire agreement. I even made a hot dish. He said it was almost as good as my chicken-fried steak. During a time of peace, we found Fremont's Point. It was two miles down the road from the house I lived in. On a splendid, autumn day we signed a purchase agreement. The strains of "Dixie" hummed in my mind.

PART III

CHAPTER 13

MYRTLE & FREMONT

Of all the log cabins in my lifetime, I would have been hard put to select a favorite. On the one hand I loved the authentic look of the weathered gray, ageless cabins along the eastern seaboard. On the other hand the warmth of the honey-colored, full pine logs of the builder's house in Longmont, Colorado spoke of the mellow feeling I was comfortable with. When the engineer and I purchased Fremont's Point, I had the best of both worlds.

The property included a cabin called "Moser's Cabin" which was built in 1907 and listed on the National Historic Register. Since a feisty lady named Myrtle outlived four husbands in that little cabin, I have always referred to the place as hers. Her furniture is there, her books are there and her records are there. It seems to me that the lady is entitled to namesake rights as well, albeit posthumously.

Louie Moser was Myrtle's second husband. He built the log cabin along with Myrtle's first husband, Fred Chandler. Since it was Louie who began operating the place as a fishing camp, the Department of Interior designated it "Moser's Cabin" in the National Historic Register listing.

Moser's Cabin was built with full logs, (seven to ten inches in diameter) set on log base plates using vertical construction. The interior logs were covered with thick, rough plaster. Data substantiating the historical status credited the vertical log style to French fur-trappers who settled in the area in the 1800's. A structure which bears a remarkable resemblance to Moser's Cabin is illustrated in Peter N. Moogk's publication, "Building a House in New France" (pub. McClelland and Steward Limited, Canada - 1977). The structure is an example of a "piquet" hut found in French fishing settlements in Newfoundland and Cape Breton. The "piquets" were popular at the early eighteenth century, therefore Louie Moser was more than a century out of context at the time he built the cabin. Since Louie was of French Canadian descent, it is assumed that he was familiar with the vertical style of construction found in Newfoundland.

Adjoining Moser's Cabin is Fremont's cabin. I never met the man, but I can guarantee you that he has good taste. He bought Myrtle's homestead in the late 60's and commenced to rebuild it. The only thing he left alone was the historic log cabin. The original cabin had an addition added in 1928 - a frame-constructed, bedroom annex. Since that didn't fit with the antiquity of the place, Fremont removed it and built his own cabin where the bedroom stood. In the corner between Myrtle's cabin and Fremont's cabin stands a huge basswood tree, massive enough to shade both log cabins. It bears a remarkable resemblance to the imaginary live oak trees of my twelfth summer.

Myrtle and her husbands operated the place as a resort for years. Fremont turned the resort into a private, corporate retreat for his company. It was a first-class operation managed by a year-round caretaker. Fremont's addition to the cabin was built with full, vertical logs in keeping with the original style. He spared no expense in the restoration of the cabin. He located a builder with the skills necessary to carry out the restoration in Menahga, Minnesota. Anti Hovasto had built log structures since his youth in Finland. He had considerable experience in the historical restoration of log structures including extensive work for the Wadena County Historical Society. Anti Hovasto and his men camped at Fremont's Point while accomplishing the refurbishing. They had a rollicking good time, telling stories and drinking beer around the campfire at night after a long day's work.

While the exterior of Fremont's cabin was allowed to weather to blend with the antique cabin, the interior pine logs were finished in a honey colored stain. The combination living/kitchen/dining room (commonly called a greatroom) overlooked Big Mantrap Lake with a long wall of windows. The greatroom had an open beamed, vaulted ceiling and massive, cobblestone fireplace as the focal point. The kitchen floor was slate, the decor was copper and blue. The chinking between the vertical logs was filled with a neat, vertical line of caulking which flowed in to smoothly fill and insulate the cracks. It was the house of my dreams.

The five cabins at Fremont's Point were rustic and charming. They were all rebuilt in the late '60's, easily maintained and tastefully decorated. Each cabin had a cobblestone fireplace or a Franklin wood stove as a back-up for the electric baseboard heating. All the cabins were wood paneled, had an abundance of windows and magnificent views of Big Mantrap Lake. The pine, polished floors had bright, braided rugs. Tab-top, cotton curtains hung on heavy, wooden dowel rods at the windows. The cabins looked as though I had decorated them myself.

The lodge was exactly the way I pictured a Northwoods hunting camp. It was authentic and comfortable. The wood walls, log beams and waxed wood floors had scars from years of living. Massive barrel chairs, thick slabwood tables and woodbins were the predominate furnishings. Light fixtures were heavy, wooden wagon wheels fitted with electric lighting. A floor to ceiling cobblestone fireplace was the focal point. Mounted deer and fish adorned the walls. Three walls of windows overlooked Big Mantrap Lake. Located at the end of the road on a peninsula, the setting was perfect. Best of all, Fremont's Point did not have a tradition of "planned family activities".

Convincing the engineer that the corporate property could be a viable business operation was one of the harder sales jobs I ever tackled. He obviously knew it would be a tough row to hoe, even if we did manage to keep the ceasefire. He went to California to finish a job assignment. I moved in at Fremont's Point.

One of the attractions to Big Mantrap Lake was the quality of the surrounding lake property. The lake was not highly developed and the property owners were not what you'd classify as "local color". They were mostly professional people. Some were retired. Many were summer residents who lived and worked elsewhere for nine months of the year. Most of the property owners were environmentally conscious people who worked at maintaining the lake quality. I met many of them while living in the house up the road. They all talked of a neighboring lake property owner named Mac.

Mac was something of a legend in his own right amongst the lake property owners. They joked about making payments and paying taxes on Mac's property. According to them, he had sole homestead, territorial, self-proclaimed rights to the entire Big Mantrap lakeshore. The legendary Mac sounded as though he might possibly be what you could term "local color". However, since I had never had the pleasure of meeting him face to face I had no way of knowing firsthand.

My introduction to Mac came the day I moved to Fremont's Point. I contracted the departing caretaker to move my furniture from the house up the road. He said that Mac had a big, blue wood-hauling truck that he might be able to use. I had seen the blue, wood-hauling truck often during the past nine months when I met it on our road. The driver never even waved to me.

Mac introduced himself with an apology for ignoring my presence for such a long time. It certainly hadn't been a neighborly thing to do. He said his avoiding me was due to the fact that there had been a long line of renters in the place where I lived. It got to be more trouble than it was worth, getting neighborly, when the renters moved right away. He figured helping me move was a fair payback for being so anti-social.

Mac didn't mince words with me right from the start. He said what he thought straight out, without bothering with social graces like tact or consideration for my feelings. He told me right away that I'd never generate enough income as a resort to pay my property taxes. According to him, he should know since he was a retired resorter by the time he was in his thirties. Obviously he knew more about my business than I did.

While you couldn't classify Mac as "local color", he did look like he belonged exactly where he was. He was a hardy, ruddy-faced woodsman, with dark, graying hair and a well trimmed beard. With ice and snow clinging to his beard, he bore a striking resemblance to the abominable snowman.

Since Mac was a few years younger than me, he was a success story in how to retire at an early age. Of course he wasn't what you would call "retired". He had a full-time job telling us all how to maintain his/our property and protect his/our environment. He took his job seriously. The fact that he didn't know me well didn't keep him from bossing me around. Sometimes I took his bossing, sometimes I didn't. Mac reminded me of a cross between the engineer and my mother. It was apparent that he had never spent any time with either of them. He didn't even bother to preface his orders with, "Now, Larren, etc."

It was Christmas time (less than two weeks after my dad's funeral) that I moved into my third log cabin. My first night at Fremont's Point was quite memorable. I fell into bed sometime after midnight, exhausted from a long day of packing and moving. A full moon was shining through the sliding, glass patio door of my bedroom. The moonlight shimmered on the frozen, snow-covered lake outside the door. It was a beautiful setting. It would be even more breathtaking when the ice left the lake in the spring. The solitude was peaceful. I was content. With a start, my peaceful solitude was broken by shadowy figures making their way alongside the house. The shadows became larger as they approached the glass door of my bedroom. I was alone at the end of the road. Frightened and not daring to make a sound, I reached for the loaded twenty-two rifle under my bed. It was my dad's squirrel gun that I carried to the door. It had not been fired since his last shot. I didn't know if I remembered how to fire the gun. I waited in silence to meet whoever came to the door. I heard footsteps as they crunched in the crusty snow, closer and louder with each step. I took a long breath, cocked the trigger and assured myself that I was capable of shooting any intruder. Seconds seemed like an eternity as I waited in the darkness. Finally, I came face to face with the intruders. I breathed a sigh of relief as I looked through the glass door at three of the most beautiful deer I have ever seen.

After the deer episode, I felt safe and comfortable in the house at the end of the road. It seemed like home from the first day I was there. I needed the sturdy, massive, log beams and the crackling, birch logs in the fireplace as much for emotional stability as I did for warmth. I sat for hours gazing at the pine log walls and the crackling fire, keeping company with my memories. Then I sat for hours reading Myrtle's books and records. I marveled at the tenacity of the woman. As her records told the story of her struggle to provide her son with life's necessities, she reminded me of my mother. I remembered the butter she churned, the bread she baked and the eggs she sold as I read the accounts in Myrtle's ledger.

My mother is one of the most determined women I have ever known when she puts her mind to something. Whether I acquired her tenacity as I tagged after her or from her genetic make-up, she is without a doubt the source of my tenacious spirit. Her tenacity has served me well. It has seen me through many an uphill battle.

Since the one thing Daddy lacked was patience, it was Mother who taught me whatever I needed to be taught. Driving was no exception. At the age of fourteen, I got my learner's driving permit. Mother and I got in the family hog truck. We practiced in the hayfield, on the road to the mailbox and other less frequently traveled roads. Finally, we advanced to the highways. This was in the days when the highways were not four-lane freeways. There was room for two cars to meet and pass, but the bridges were not built as wide as the highways. You had to slow down and watch your fenders if you met another car on a bridge.

One of the worst bridges I ever drove across spanned the Arkansas River outside of Fort Smith, Arkansas. It happened to be the first bridge I ever drove across. When we approached that particular bridge, I assumed we would change drivers and my mother would drive us safely across. She got that steely, Messer gleam in her eye and said, "Now, Larren, whenever you come face to face with an obstacle in life, you don't ever back down. You cross that bridge."

I crossed that bridge on high. I gunned that hog truck and I sailed over that bridge so fast it made your head spin. By the time we reached the other side of the bridge, Mother's steely, Messer gleam was a bit glazed. The woman never flinched and I never backed down. Not then and not ever.

I remembered my mother's words as I settled in at the log cabin in the Minnesota northwoods. I would draw on her tenacity many times that winter. Building a commercial resort operation was an uphill struggle all the way. The engineer was in California my first winter at the resort. The snow got deeper and deeper. I shoveled cabin rooftops and learned to plow snow with the best of them. I whipped that Jeep snowplow through the drifts and around the curves. It was similar to the hog truck. I imagined there was a red-faced Irishman looking on and cackling. Perhaps it was only Mac's laughter that I heard.

I will be the first to admit there were times when I needed Mac's help and advice that first winter. When I needed him, it was in a somewhat desperate, dire time of need. Either I had frozen something or flooded something or plugged something up. When I did, I headed up the road to Mac's house. It was bad enough that I had to beg. Having to do it in person, face to face, was even more humiliating. Mac refused to join the outside world with a telephone. It seems that he had his fill of telephones during his resorting days. Being as how he was surrounded by neighbors of the "city slicker" variety, he did not choose to be forever summoned to our rescue with a telephone. I had to really need Mac's help to go to the trouble of hunting him down.

Sometimes I figured hunting him down was more trouble than it was worth. Then I proceeded with whatever needed to be done all by myself. I learned many valuable lessons as a result. Sometimes it was just too embarrassing to have to own up to whatever it was I had messed up. Mac seemed to have an uncanny way of being right in his predictions. I would have made my resort business succeed just to prove Mac wrong.

Spring finally came and so did the business. On week-ends, so did the engineer. He worked a job in Minneapolis through the week. It was Calgary all over again. I dreaded week-ends. The ceasefire didn't last. It was Vicksburg and Gettysburg, Antietam and Atlanta. Our word battles raged on. We talked of divorce and the conversation got to settlement terms.

Now here was where push came to shove. The engineer figured that since he had been off at these God-forsaken outposts earning the money, he deserved the spoils. I figured that since I had invested money with good, Southern roots I wasn't about to let some damned Yankee have it. I could trace that money right back to its third generation twice removed, way back to when Ace and I worked his way through college thirty years before. It was truly amazing, the genetic history of that money.

The engineer and I finally parted, ten years after we moved from Spindly Pines Drive. Our version of the Civil War had no winners or losers - only survivors. He went west, back to engineering. I heard he married and was happy. I'd lay you odds the lady in question did not spring from Southern roots. I stayed in the log cabin and built a thriving resort business. Like my mother always said, "All's well that ends well."

Mac has remained my unsolicited, unpaid quality control man for six years now. He has trained me in many areas. He has cleaned up my messes ranging from fallen trees to backed-up sewers. He provides me with handmade log benches, clean wood duck nesting boxes, recycled clothes and magazines, any bargain he finds and more free advice than I can handle. He continues to lecture me on the best management practices concerning the lake, the woods, my resort and my life. Mac can be one of the most obstinate people I have ever known when he sets his mind to something.

My mother would say, "That's like the pot calling the kettle black." (Me calling Mac obstinate.) It is a love/hate relationship that Mac and I have. He loves to be right, I hate to be wrong.

Just as I suspected all along, the rest of the neighbors are a fairly bland assortment of professional people - totally lacking in "local color".

EPILOGUE

THE AGGIE & THE OKIE

I first met the Aggie shortly after I moved to northern Minnesota. Of course I didn't know he was an Aggie then. He was a university professor in the field of hospitality and tourism promotion. He talked pretty good Northern and wore a suit and tie and in no way, shape or form resembled an Aggie. He was so cooly professional, I assumed he had to be a bonafide Yankee. I gave him a wide berth. I'd had enough of Yankees trying to tell me how to run a resort. I was doing just fine with good old Southern hospitality. I didn't need any advice from Yankee professors. To tell the truth, I didn't much care for the Yankee professor.

The first time I had any dealings with the professor occurred while I was promoting tourism to the North country. Since he was a respected authority, I contracted him and his colleagues to do a series of seminars on tourism. I was in the process of buying Fremont's Point. When he heard what I was up to, he told me he had looked at the property himself. He dismissed the notion after doing a feasibility study and deciding it was not a feasible business prospect. Of course I couldn't have cared less if it was feasible or not.

143

The property had not one but two log cabins combined. That was feasible enough to suit me. I would show that *#!* Yankee professor a thing or two about feasibility.

The next time I saw the professor he was wearing Levis, cowboy boots and a snap-button western shirt. At first I didn't recognize him out of uniform. I assumed he was on his way to a masquerade party. We chatted. He asked about my feasible business operation. I took a great deal of pride in telling him it was coming along just fine, thank you. My favorite words have always been, "I told you so."

The Yankee professor was looking for resorts to tour with his university class. He assumed I had plenty of vacancies. A few weeks later he arrived at Fremont's Point with his students, still wearing his party clothes. I figured Yankee professors must take masquerade balls more seriously than most people do. His outfit was appropriate, however, since I was also wearing Levis and a denim shirt. It was what I always wore when I did resort work.

The first inkling I had that the professor wasn't a bonafide Yankee happened quite by chance. I served a meal of homemade biscuits, fried pork chops and cream gravy. The professor said, "Why, I haven't had a good, Southern meal like this in a coon's age." I was totally taken aback! I hadn't heard the expression "in a coon's age" since my Grandad Messer died.

I questioned that phony Yankee professor right away about where he heard that "coon's age" expression. It seems that he had lived a good portion of his life in

Texas. He attended college at Nacogdoches and earned his Ph.D. from Texas A.& M. at College Station. Later on, he had raised cows near Fort Worth, Texas.

Now to understand the significance of this, you have to understand that to an Okie a Texas Aggie is about as lowdown as a Yankee. Aggies are to Okies what sheepmen are to cow people or the Hatfields are to the McCoys. Okies do not take kindly to Texas Aggies. The only thing worse that he could have possibly been was from the University of Texas. The O.U. vs. Texas football rivalry is a blood feud between the Sooners and the Longhorns that has spoiled many a possible friendship.

After the ice was broken with the "coon's age" expression, I softened somewhat to the Aggie/Yankee professor. At least I knew how to handle a man with good Southern roots. It was rather refreshing to talk to someone who spoke my language. It did, however, have a devastating effect on my own effort to speak pretty good Northern. Linguistically speaking, we brought out the "you all" in each other. We had much in common including two divorces and cornbread dressing. He had struggled with two mixed marriages with Yankee wives. As long as he kept his feasibility feelings regarding my resort to himself, I reckoned that I could show him a bit of down home, Southern hospitality.

From time to time the Aggie stopped by the resort, just to see how my business was coming. He said it was a professional interest. Of course he wasn't fooling me one bit. I knew all along that my homemade biscuits, fried pork chops and cream gravy were the real reasons the Aggie kept coming back. However, I took a great deal of satisfaction in showing off my business to him. I'd worked hard to attract guests. I figured I was entitled to flaunt them.

I have to give that Aggie credit. He did know when to keep his professorial opinions to himself. Not once did he ever say, "Now, Larren, you have to, etc." It just goes to show that Aggies have more sense than Okies give them credit for.

While I enjoyed listening to the Aggie's Southern drawl, I did have a bit of a problem regarding his wearing apparel. During my dating years, wearing cowboy boots and snap-button shirts was equal to driving a hog truck. It was reason enough to say no. I spent my entire life trying to get my daddy and my brother out of their cowboy boots and snap-button shirts. I never did. The closest I had ever come to a snap-button shirt was every Christmas when I wrapped them as gifts for my daddy. Now here I was keeping company with a man in a snap-button, western shirt. I could understand why the actress had been so concerned about her sister when she considered buying one of the things. It was an unsettling thing and totally out of character. The most unsettling thing of all was the overwhelming feeling that I had come home.

The professor left the north country to accept a position at a university in New Mexico not a hundred miles from the adobe from my past. He loved it as much as I did. It seemed that we had more and more in common; our past, our present and finally our future. At first the Aggie became my business partner and later my husband. Our lawyer said it was a fairly binding pre-nuptial agreement that we had. My mother said, "The third time's the charm."

The wedding was in the summertime, so as to avoid the bride slipping on the ice in her wedding finery. The groom was handsome in his cowboy boots, Levis and snap-button shirt. Mac took the wedding pictures. The Yankee who performed the courthouse ceremony said he used SuperGlue, so as to avoid any more divorces. The bride hummed "Dixie" in her mind.

After three years in New Mexico, the professor retired from university teaching. We came home to live full-time in our log cabin in the Minnesota northwoods. While we shared a love for history and Myrtle's cabin, the Aggie felt that Fremont's cabin was a trifle ostentatious. He said he felt more comfortable in a more modest cabin. When he came to realize that biscuits and gravy were only served in the ostentatious log cabin, he came to feel quite comfortable there.

The Aggie and I work well together. He reminds me of all the most important men throughout my life. I see much of my dad, my grandad, my brother and Ace - all in the Aggie. I sometimes wish there was more than a glimpse of the engineer, since the Aggie's carpentry is "hell for stout, but not much for pretty". His description, not mine. It's hard to teach an old dog new tricks. I continue to try.

I remind the Aggie of his mother, his grandmother, his daughter and the college sweetheart who refused to go north of the Red River with him. He approves of my tight blue jeans and enjoys my Southern cooking. He calls cornbread "Johnny Cake" and eats it with honey. I figure he's only trying to beat me at my own game, trying to be more Southern than me. We share a culture, a heritage and a love for the north country. The Aggie more closely resembles a Jackpine Savage than a professor these days.

When our fishing resort guests talk of bucktails and spinner baits, the Aggie and I recall fishing in the farm ponds of our youth. Back then, our tackle was a willow switch and a string with a washer tied on for a sinker. We either dug grubworms from a dried manure pile in the cow lot or chased grasshoppers in the cow pasture for bait. We laugh that the spouse we located in northern Minnesota knows about grubworms in cowpiles and grasshoppers and willow switches.

We are one of the more well informed fishing resorts. The Aggie spends two hours each and every day of his life watching the local and national news. We are up to the minute with our coverage, whether the lead stories pertain to war, crime or politics. In northern Minnesota, the lead stories often pertain to fishing.

The Aggie and I live quietly and simply as small resort owners do. We are happy and healthy and don't ask much more. Most of the year we delight in the clear water and loon music of Big Mantrap Lake. We watch eagles soar over the lofty pines and breathe deeply of the pure northwoods air. We delight in the glories of autumn and the first snowfalls of winter. We cut two Christmas trees from our woods and drag them across the frozen lake to our log cabins. Log cabins are at their best during the Christmas season when decorated with the festive holiday reds and greens. We ski and ice fish and sit by the fire.

When we have tired of shoveling snow and bundling in layers of coats and mittens, we pack our gear in the hog truck. We head for south Texas across the Red River. We stop at any restaurant that features Mexican cooking, real Texas barbecue or Louisiana Cajun to eat our fill of the foods from our past. We talk Dixie and say "you all" to our heart's content. We count our blessings while we share both the worlds we love with a kindred spirit.

As for proverbs, they fly fast and furiously in our household. The one that seems to suit the situation comes from the mother of a dear friend who is a hardy, northwoods soul herself.

"For every bent pot, there's a bent lid."
(Lorelei's Mother)

From time to time the Aggie and I talk of retirement and where we want to be in ten or twenty years. He talks of south Texas and eastern Oklahoma. We consider New Mexico. The Aggie loves to look at property for sale. I humor him and tag along. I know deep in my heart that I will spend the rest of my life in Fremont's and Myrtle's log cabins. Old love affairs die hard. I smile at the Aggie in the snap-button shirt.

The strains of "Dixie" hum in my mind.

149